Giftbringer

THE STORY OF YOUNG ST. NICHOLAS

BY

Frederick Wiegand

TATE PUBLISHING, LLC

Published in the United States of America

By TATE PUBLISHING, LLC

All rights reserved.
Do not duplicate without permission.
All Scripture references are King James Version,
unless otherwise indicated.
Book Design by TATE PUBLISHING, LLC.
Printed in the United States of America by

TATE PUBLISHING, LLC

127 East Trade Center Terrace

Mustang, OK 73064

(888) 361-9473

Publisher's Cataloging in Publication

Wiegand, Frederick

Giftbringer / Frederick Wiegand

Originally published in Mustang,OK:TATE PUBLISHING:2004

1. Christmas 2. Fiction - Historical

ISBN 1-9331482-7-6 $19.95

Copyright 2004

First Printing: December 2004

This story about giving
is dedicated to
someone very special
who has a loving and giving heart
and gives generously of herself
to her many friends and loved ones—

ROBERTA HOLT SACHS
"Aunt Bobbe"

TABLE OF CONTENTS

" . . . the stockings were hung by the chimney with care,
in the hope that St. Nicholas soon would be there."

—Clement Clarke Moore
"A Visit from St. Nicholas," 1822

" . . . therefore, Christian men, be sure,
wealth and rank possessing,
ye who now will bless the poor
shall yourselves find blessing."

—Old English Carol
"Good King Wenceslas," 1582

FOREWORD

In his story of *Giftbringer,* author Frederick Wiegand takes us to the legendary origin of good old St. Nick. Beginning with his upbringing and giving us insight into his parents and the values that they tried to instill in this young man, we follow a story that teaches us about jealousy and envy, discontentment, and gratitude. We encounter young Nicolas as the author draws us into his relationship with his best friend, Petrus. Then we all travel on a journey together as the two discover young manhood, evaluate true convictions, and pursue happiness, careers, and love.

The challenges of balancing the emotions that come between love and career allow us to search along with the two young men for the true meaning of life. The twists and turns and the hills and valleys of their relationship with each other as well as with those around them lead us to an almost soap opera type of vortex, but this is where we begin to fully understand the giving heart that motivates the exploits of Nicolas. We are only allowed enough time to exhale before Wiegand introduces another subplot that entices us to discover how it unfolds. With a few, very clever twists, Wiegand lets us know that this is just the beginning of many more adventures of Nicolas.

I found *Giftbringer* to be compelling reading. The subplots made it very difficult for me to put the book down until I could arrive at a break in the action. I shared many of the chapters with my children and my wife. God has blessed me with four daughters, who took such an avid interest in the story that eventually I would search for the book only to find it in one of their rooms. We would discuss the plots together and try to guess how each episode would develop. If my experiences are any indication, *Giftbringer* will prove to be a great book for the entire family. It will allow parents and children to discuss some of life's issues and compare notes on how they feel about the questions raised by the trials and temptations faced by Nicolas in the difficult process of growing up.

Wiegand has introduced a series of chronicles of Nicolas that I truly believe will be around for a long, long time. A classic in its own right, *Giftbringer* is a great gift to share with someone special. If you enjoy reading stories of love, adventure, and challenge, accompanied by deeper meaning and strong moral principles, you will absolutely enjoy reading this novel. *Giftbringer* is a very exciting story that touches every human emotion. Wiegand takes you on a journey through time and imagination in such a way that it leaves you wanting to travel with him again and again. You will love every chapter of this thrilling story of young Nicolas, the *Giftbringer*. Read it. Enjoy it. Above all, share it.

David Cobb
Pastor, Recording Artist, and International Worship Leader
Fairfield, CA

INTRODUCTION:

The Real Santa Claus

Yes, Virginia, there was a Santa Claus. According to history and tradition, he lived during the days when the Roman Empire flourished throughout most of the known world. In those days he didn't travel around in a sleigh pulled by reindeer, nor did he live at the North Pole. He didn't manufacture childrens' toys with the assistance of elves. He didn't wear a suit made of red fur with white trim, although medieval artists sometimes depicted him in red robes. He didn't grow his long, white beard until his middle years, and although we think of him as an immortal old man, he actually had a childhood and youth like any human. Despite these differences, he did have one thing in common with "Jolly Old St. Nicholas," (as we have come to know and love him today)—he was a giftbringer.

He gave gifts at night and with great stealth. He waited until everyone in the household had gone to sleep, and then he crept inside, left his gift, and departed. His nocturnal visits were kept a secret, as he did not want the recipients to know of his generosity. At first he didn't give gifts to everyone, but only to some particularly fortunate young women. He tried his best not to let it be known that he was the mysterious benefactor. However, in spite of his attempts to keep quiet about his good works, his reputation as a friend to the poor and the have-nots quickly grew and spread. Even during his own lifetime, people considered Nicholas a saint.

What makes a person a giver? How does a man gain a reputation that grows from generation to generation until he becomes known as the greatest gift-giver of all time? What causes an individual to put the well-being of others ahead of his own personal needs? This is the kind of fundamental inquiry from which the following narrative grew. It was meant as a parable of the relationship between human beings and material goods, as a fable depicting a human heart's transformation from selfishness to selflessness.

All of the sources tell that Nicholas was the son of wealthy, somewhat elderly parents. This information is nearly all that is known of his early life, though some accounts include the parents' names and imply that their wealth was inherited due to their being of noble birth. How then, I wondered, could a child from a wealthy family, presumably raised with every luxury at his fingertips, choose to give instead of to take? Why did he choose to dedicate his life to benefiting others, when he could have grown up spoiled and selfish? The simple answer, of course, is his parents. They were good people, they were Christians, and they raised him in an environment of giving. This much is implied in the original story. Having grown up in a household of love, he naturally developed a heart for loving and giving to others, and he proceeded to live out what he had been taught. It's a very tidy solution. Perhaps a little too tidy.

Life is a series of reverses and contraries, of ups and downs, and of backwards and forwards. Not everything manages to go exactly as intended. A person's career may begin in one part of the world and in one profession, and by the time the same person retires, his or her pathway may have taken so many twists and turns that he or she ends in another locale and in a completely different vocation. A young rail-splitter from Kentucky becomes President of the United States. A boy growing up on a Missouri farm turns out to be the creator of the most famous animated cartoons in the world. A rejected New York showgirl whose talents are considered questionable at best eventually is known as the all-time queen of television comedy. Just as life seldom goes in a straightforward, predictable progression, so are human beings quirky, unreliable, and absolutely unpredictable. An expensive best-selling toy that heads every child's wish list one Christmas may, by the next year, wind up on the bargain table at the lowest price possible. Even in Biblical times, the same crowd that welcomed Jesus into Jerusalem with palm branches was crying out for His blood a few days later.

So it may have been with the boy Nicholas. What if, I wondered, he did not start out as a giver? What if he did not necessarily agree with his parents' philosophy of putting others first? What if, before he knew generosity, he underwent a painful growing-up process during which he struggled with his natural selfishness, and learned only with some difficulty that it is indeed "more blessed to give than to receive"? What if he, in fact, had been human?

This line of questioning caused the following tale to unfold. The sources are both history and legend. The characters are based on the little that is known of that nobly-born young man who lived so long ago. How much is based on factual or source material, and how much is the writer's own fabrication? The more improbable parts are the true ones. For the details, it was necessary to add and invent. The character of Petrus is a creation of the author, but he has his origin in the St. Nicholas mythos. Those familiar with European tradition will recognize at once the transmogrified figure of Black Peter, the saint's companion who delivers the switches and the coal to unworthy children. The daughters, of course, are part of the original story, as is their father and his encounter with St. Nicholas. The princes were a necessary addition in order to flesh out the story of the Dowerless Maidens.

Liberties have been taken in the historical accuracy which has frequently been sacrificed for the purposes of storytelling. Since the chief sources on Nicholas, primarily *The Golden Legend,* date from the Middle Ages, the late Roman setting is covered with a medieval gloss. For example, priestly celibacy was not a requirement until slightly later in church history, but by the time the legends of Nicholas were written down, it had become an established tradition. In the present narrative it was used to sharpen the contrast between a worldly existence and a religious life. Another example is that nowhere in the original account of the legend does it suggest that St. Nicholas' nocturnal visits occurred at Christmastime. In fact the association with Christmas during the saint's lifetime is rather tenuous. However, his reputation over the centuries has become so firmly linked with that particular holiday, it seemed expedient to set the gift-giving against the background of the observance of the birth of Christ. Another juggling of dates occurs in the establishment of December sixth as Nicholas' birthday. In actuality, this date, which is commemorated in some countries as part of the celebration of Christmas, is traditionally associated with St. Nicholas' death. However, as it is not completely unheard of for people to die on their birthdays, and lacking any other information about the real date of birth, I used it as the most appropriate alternative. Finally, the Fortunatus purse probably did not yet exist in that early era. However, as it tied in nicely with the theme and made a good object lesson for the boy Nicholas, I included it without further inquiry into its place in history.

As for the rest of the story, I followed the blueprints laid out for me by the original legends and my own personal line of inquiry. Once the characters and main idea were in place, the story followed its natural course. If it seems at the end to beg for a sequel, this is because it was originally to have been one small section of a tiny book designed to fit easily inside a Christmas stocking. The book was to cover the saint's life and the miracles that continued long after his death. Needless to say, it grew from there. Instead of covering the events of the saint's entire life and in order to maintain unity of time, place, and character, the focus has been narrowed to that of Nicholas' childhood and his young manhood. Even though it was originally planned to stretch over a greater period of time, the present work is designed to stand on its own.

So, though neither a slim volume nor a comprehensive biography, *Giftbringer* is an attempt to explain how the most famous giver of gifts grew into his reputation. If it seems to be a stretch from sleigh bells and reindeer, remember that this is but the beginning of a long journey. This is the story of what really happened. Or rather, it is the story of what *might* have really happened.

CHARACTERS

EPHANUS PROSPERIOS,
a wealthy Greek nobleman of Patara

JOANA, his wife, of East Slavic descent

NICOLAS, their son

SERGIUS MAXIMUS, a retired Roman senator

PRISCILA, his very young Moorish wife

PETRUS, their son

ABBOT STEPHANUS,
head of the local monastic order and
younger brother of EPHANUS

FLORUS DORIUS, another wealthy nobleman

ANGELINA, his eldest daughter

ABIGAIL, his second daughter

ANA, his third daughter

MARLA, sister of FLORUS

PRINCE KORIN KORATOVICH of Novgorod

PRINCE ILYAN KORATOVICH,
younger brother of PRINCE KORIN

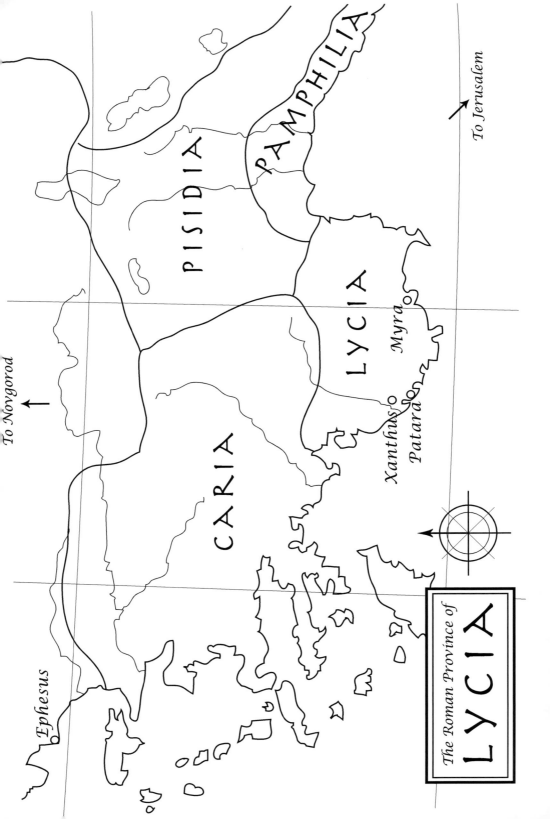

To Novgorod

To Jerusalem

PISIDIA

PAMPHILIA

CARIA

LYCIA

Myra

Xanthus

Patara

Ephesus

The Roman Province of
LYCIA

SETTING

The city of Patara in the country of Lycia, a part of Asia Minor, in what is now known as Turkey. The year is 270 A.D. The Roman Empire governs most of the known world, and Lycia is one of its provinces.

A Prayer is a Wish Your Heart Makes

Joana stood on the balcony and stared up at the night sky.

"Joana, why are you out here? We have guests." Ephanus drew aside the curtain and stepped outside to put a hand on his wife's shoulder.

A tear sparkled in the moonlight as it trickled down her face. "I was feeling unwell, a trifle dizzy. It will pass. I just needed some air."

"How long have you been having these ill feelings?" asked Ephanus, in concern.

"Only for a few days. I'm sure it is nothing," said Joana. She sighed and gazed again at the stars.

"Something else is troubling you," discerned Ephanus. "Won't you tell me what it is? Is it something to do with our guests?"

Joana sighed, knowing that Ephanus' concern for her was so great that she would have to tell him sooner or later. "Priscila's child comes in the spring," she said.

"That is cause for rejoicing, not for tears," said Ephanus. "Should we not be happy in the happiness of my greatest friend and his wife?"

"It is hard to sit listening to her as she talks of it, knowing that you and I will probably never have a child of our own. She is much younger than I," said Joana.

"But not half as beautiful," said Ephanus, gently wiping away the tiny tear from her eye.

Joana turned her face away until the shadows obscured it. "I am long past my fortieth year," she said. "There are rings under my eyes and lines on my forehead. How could you call me beautiful?"

"Your inner beauty shines forth and keeps your face fresh and young in my eyes," said Ephanus. "I loved you when we married, and I love you more now because I know you so much better. As a wife, you have always fulfilled my every desire." He caressed her shoulder tenderly as he spoke these words.

She shook her head sadly. "Not every desire," she said. "You may be one of the wealthiest men in all of Lycia, and I as your wife may share in all of your worldly goods, but in one respect we are the poorest people on earth."

"It is true that I, too, have longed for a child as much as you, but if it has pleased God to keep us childless, we cannot argue. Besides, there is always hope."

"Hope?" asked Joana. "I am now closer to fifty than to forty, and you, my lord, are five years older than I. How can it be that we shall ever be blessed with a child of our own?"

"God performs miracles," said Ephanus. "We must hold onto our faith, and we must trust in Him to listen to our prayers. And we must keep trying. I have not given up on this matter, and neither should you. God will bless our efforts to have a child."

"I haven't a prayer left inside me," said Joana. "When I see how happy Priscila is, it only makes my pain greater."

"Tomorrow," promised Ephanus, "we will go to my brother's chapel and pray for a child. I still have prayers left in me, and I will help you to pray. Now, dry those tears and come back to our guests."

"Yes, Ephanus," said Joana. "I will." Turning to take one

last look at the night sky, Joana suddenly clutched her husband's toga and drew him toward her. "Look, look, Ephanus!" she exclaimed. "Look at that star!"

A streak of light shot across the sky.

"A shooting star! Do you know what this means, Ephanus? It means our prayer is to be answered! I know it! I just know it!"

"Then we must be sure to go to prayer tomorrow. Come in now out of the cool night air," said Ephanus.

At the entry, as Ephanus held the curtain for her to pass under it, she closed her eyes and sank into his arms. She appeared to have lost consciousness.

He placed her on their bed. On the verge of sending one of the servants to fetch a doctor, he felt relief when she opened her eyes and smiled at him.

"Don't forget about going to prayer tomorrow," she said.

"I won't. We must pray for a child, and now for your good health as well. Your dizziness and fainting have me worried. I must offer every supplication to God."

"No," said Joana. "We must give thanks instead."

Her husband could only answer with a puzzled expression.

"Don't you see?" asked Joana. "My late illnesses have only been a symptom of something greater. I didn't consider it possible until this moment, but now I think our prayer has already been answered!"

* * * * * *

On a Monday, the sixth day of December, Joana gave birth to a son. She had never known such joy in her life as that which she experienced during the nine months of her pregnancy. She had endured every discomfort with a cheerful, thankful heart. A deep sense of gratitude toward God filled her soul every day, from the night she had first known of her expected child to the morning of the delivery. She named her son Nicolas, which means "victorious."

By her bedside stood Ephanus, who had held her hand all during the trauma of giving birth. The doctors had all departed— Joana's husband had brought in the best doctors that money could buy to assist in the process, so that his wife's every need could be taken care of as far as was humanly possible. Ephanus' best friend Sergius and his young Moorish wife Priscila stood on the other side of the bed. Priscila held her seven-month-old boy Petrus, wrapped in gold cloth.

"God is truly good," said Joana.

Ephanus noticed that his friend winced slightly. Sergius did not believe in Christianity, nor in the concept of one God, and thus religion had long been a bone of contention between them. Ephanus did not allow this difference in opinion to stand in the way of their friendship, however, as the two had grown up together and had been almost constant companions for nearly fifty years. Sergius, if he worshiped at all, followed the old Roman gods and wondered why his friend chose a new faith that until recent years had had to be practiced in secret. Sergius knew that Ephanus had recognized his wince and had understood the reason for it. He felt uncomfortable every time his friend or his friend's wife invoked the God of an unauthorized religion.

As if in confirmation of his mother's statement, the infant broke free from Joana's arms and stood, unaided, on the bed, wrapped only in layers of soft cloth. He spread his arms out wide and looked up to Heaven. A beam of light broke through the grey clouds and shone through the nearby window, bathing the child in a golden glow.

Joana gasped. Sergius rubbed his eyes, shook his head, then looked again. Priscilla's eyes opened wide with wonder, making her face appear more youthful and childlike than ever. Even baby Petrus, gazing in silence, seemed to have gotten wrapped up in the spell of the moment. Only Ephanus evinced no shock or surprise, as his belief in the miraculous had never faltered.

The sunbeam soon got swallowed up by a cloud, and the child sank once more into his mother's loving embrace. All became as it had been.

"If I hadn't seen it," murmured Priscila, "I would never have believed it!"

"I *don't* believe it," announced Sergius. "Some trick of the light caused us to imagine we saw something impossible. I hope you will not mention this hallucination to anyone else."

"It was a miracle," said Joana.

Ephanus took his wife's hand and said nothing. No words existed to express what thoughts and feelings filled his mind and heart.

CHAPTER ONE:

A Rich Man

Market day in Patara took on the air of a festival. Merchants bedecked their carts with brightly-colored ribbons and filled the market square with their hawking cries. The exotic mingled with the commonplace. Fresh fruits, fresh vegetables, and bread taken piping hot from the oven could be purchased at a good price, along with more expensive merchandise such as perfumes from India, herbs, jewels, and spices from Arabia, and fine woven cloth from China. Merchants from the neighboring countries of Greece to the west and the Slavic lands to the north brought wares and foods unique to their particular climes. Other merchants came from as far away as Egypt or Persia. Not only did the merchants arrive in droves, but all of Lycia, or so it seemed, came forth to buy, sell, bargain, beg, or simply watch.

Beggars in tattered rags moaned feebly with outstretched hands. Musicians played on lyres, flutes, or sitars. Beautiful dark-skinned women performed exotic dances for a fee. Housewives haggled over prices of crockery. Horse traders quarreled over the age and condition of a mare or stallion. Rug dealers tried to undersell each other. Deals closed or went unmade. Hands shook. Purses opened. Coins exchanged hands. Merchant and customer alike parted grinning, each certain he had gotten the best of the bargain. Other customers walked away from vendors cursing, threatening never to do further business with that seller, at least until the next week when prices would be raised or lowered and the process would start all over again.

Joana went from stall to stall with a large wicker basket in her hands, seeking the freshest fruits and vegetables for the best prices. Ephanus bartered over a choice goose and other meats. Nicolas, waiting patiently, carried a great sack, to the contents of which his parents continually added their purchases. Though only seven years of age, he had already developed great strength in his arms from carrying these loads on a weekly basis.

Young Nicolas had inherited the golden hair and fair skin that had been his mother's in her youth, and from his father he received the grave, earnest, grey eyes that occasionally twinkled with mirth but generally held pity, compassion, and love for his fellow man within their expressive depths. The boy seldom smiled, but when he did his entire face lit up with a warm radiance. He had a peaceful, friendly, and outgoing disposition, but he also had a temper that could flare up unexpectedly. This Joana feared he had gotten from her, for her husband Ephanus never showed the slightest outburst of anger or even momentary irritation, whereas she herself had only a modicum of patience and tended to get frustrated at even the smallest matters. Tempers aside, she rested in the knowledge that if anyone could teach Nicolas self-governance it was the strict yet patient Ephanus.

The sack had begun to feel extremely heavy, but Nicolas offered no complaint. The weekly ritual had become such a matter of custom that the boy never thought much about it one way or the other. He guessed that other families did much the same as his own, and since he had known no other family he had nothing with which to compare his own routine. If anything, he took pride and pleasure in helping his parents in their good works, although he did sometimes wonder if this was all there would ever be to life.

Breaking free from his transaction with the butcher, Ephanus hustled to the spot where his son awaited him. He carried not only the prize goose, but three pheasants as well. His cheery smile and brisk movements conveyed evidence, if any were needed, of the supreme pleasure he took in personally providing for the poor.

"Wonderful news, Nico. I have gotten these birds for a third of their normal cost, as they are more than a day old." Greeting his son effusively and ruffling the boy's golden hair, Ephanus waved to his wife, who had just likewise completed her business and now approached them, her basket brimming with fresh produce. "Good prices?" he called, and she nodded eagerly, stepping up her pace as she crossed the market square.

Nicolas noticed a lean boy, with a face like a hungry wolf, emerging from among the crowd. Before anyone could give warning, the boy snatched a melon from Joana's basket and fled down the street.

"Come back here!" screamed Nicolas, setting down his sack and pursuing the thief.

"Now, Nico," said Ephanus, gently reaching out a hand to restrain his son. "It's all right. Don't worry about it." But his boy had already run off.

"Nico! Nico!" shouted Joana, as her son dashed past her.

Nicolas ran down the street, following the thief, who led him on a merry chase, first heading in one direction and then another. The chase ended quickly, however, as the thief rounded a corner and then melted into the throng. Frustrated, Nicolas could go no further in pursuit. Tears of hot anger stung his eyes.

Not only had the thief eluded him, he no longer knew where he was, having turned so many corners that he now stood in a section of town unfamiliar to him.

"Will you give a coin to a poor beggar?" whined a voice near his feet. Looking down, Nicolas beheld an old man with shriveled skin and practically no teeth, dressed in tattered cloth. On further observation, Nicolas realized with a shock that the man was not really old, but only looked that way, having been disfigured by years of starvation. He was a young man, maybe only a few years older than Nicolas himself. The realization and the sight before him filled the boy with pity, but also disgust. Even if he had wanted to give a coin to the man, he had none upon his person at the moment, so there was nothing he could do.

"No," said Nicolas, firmly. "No, I cannot." Then anger filled him, as he realized it was one such as this who had stolen from his mother. "No, your kind has done enough hurt for one day. Why don't you just go away?" Nicolas looked around him in desperation. Where were his parents? Could they find him? Then he cast another glance downward.

The beggar gave him a wide-eyed, hurt look, as of a puppy that had just been whipped. The expression made the young man look much younger, showing that his age might have been even less than Nicolas had, at second glance, reckoned. His hair, prematurely white, could have been the color of Nicolas' own golden curls before hunger and the elements had ravaged his young head and his face, if not so sunken and shriveled, might have resembled Nicolas' own bright-cheeked, clear complexion. Here, Nicolas suddenly realized, was someone so like himself that it was like looking into a distorted mirror. At this thought, Nicolas' eyes filled with horror, and he stumbled hastily away.

A great cheer arose from the crowded street. Having put some distance between himself and the beggar, Nicolas sought a vantage point from which he could see whoever or whatever inspired the cheering cries. He tried everything. He looked between people's legs, dropped to the ground to peer through an ocean of shoes, sandals, and bare feet, and tried to jump high enough to see over the shoulders that blocked his view. He finally clambered onto a rug merchant's cart, piled high with soft, intricately-patterned Persian rugs, while the merchant himself was distracted by the commotion in the street. From this comfortable perch, Nicolas beheld the sight that was to change his life forever.

A boy about his own age, surely a prince or young noble-man, rode in a magnificent chariot drawn by two sleek, black Arabian horses. He wore a scarlet cloak with a jeweled clasp over a plain but elegant purple toga. A circlet in the shape of a laurel wreath, with carved leaves of sparkling gold, adorned his black hair, and the boy's flashing black eyes seemed to take in every person in the appreciative throng as he waved majestically toward the people who lined the streets.

As Nicolas gazed in rapture at the magnificent spectacle, a breathless Ephanus ran up and put a hand on his shoulder. A moment later, Joana came running up after them. Nicolas' parents embraced and caressed him, yet he found himself barely able to take notice of them, for he was caught up in the sight he had just seen.

"Who is that boy, Father?" asked Nicolas, eagerly.

"That boy? Oh, he is the son of Sergius Maximus, one of my oldest friends. His name is Petrus."

"If you know him, why have I not met him before?"

"His family does not worship as we do. Nor do they live as we do. Though Sergius and I were friends for many years, we have less and less in common. He is a very rich man. He is also a high-ranking politician, formerly of the Roman Senate, now serving as a local magistrate, while I am only a member of the town council of Patara. On top of everything else, he is a wor-shiper of the pagan gods while I and my family are Christian. I do not think he and his family would care any longer to associate with us."

"Are we not rich, then?" asked Nicolas, in a disappointed tone.

"Yes, very rich," said his father, to which Joana nodded in agreement. "But we measure wealth in other ways than the Maximus family does. We value love, honor, and obedience to Christ as true riches."

"I understand that," said Nicolas, impatiently. "But is it not possible to have all of those things and still have material goods as well? Are we not as well-to-do in money matters as the Maximus family?"

Ephanus took a deep breath and then gave a hand to his son as he led him down the street to the place where they had left their purchased goods. Joana took her son's other hand.

"My son, I will not lie to you or hide the truth. Speaking strictly in terms of money, we are much wealthier than most of the people in Patara, including my best friend and his family. Despite this, I do not want you to grow up spoiled. I want you to learn that we have many things that are much more important than money, like love and happiness."

"Is that why we live in a modest house, and go about the streets on foot instead of in a chariot? Is that why our clothes are plain and simple, and not elegant?" asked Nicolas.

"My little Nico," said his mother, "you are speaking as though you do not have enough of all the good things. Do you not have a roof over your head, and plenty of food to eat? Do you not have more clothes to wear in one week than most children see in a year?"

"I'm grateful, of course," said Nicolas, "but must we live like poor people all of the time?"

"Try to understand, my son," said Ephanus, "that money is only a tool. It will not buy happiness. If you try to buy your happiness with money, you will live a life of disappointment and regret."

Nicolas remained thoughtful as he went with his parents to retrieve the bundles, which a kindly merchant had agreed to look after until they returned.

"That thief got away with the melon," grumbled Nicolas. "He should have been caught and punished. Now he has a full belly and will steal again."

"The boy needed it more than we did," said Ephanus soothingly. "It was wrong of him to take it, but he stole because he was hungry. There are many, many people who do not have the money to buy food, and they are forced to solve the problem in whatever way they can. I do not begrudge that boy the melon. I only wish he had asked instead of taking it."

"Father, do you never become angry with anyone?" asked Nicolas, with a touch of exasperation in his tone.

"Only with those who, knowing what is right, put themselves ahead of others."

Nicolas had no response to this, so he followed his parents silently as they made their way through the streets of Patara carrying their bundles.

CHAPTER TWO:

A Poor Man

The Roman Empire up to that time had never officially recognized Christianity as a legal religion, and therefore the handling of this popular yet perplexing faith had been left up to each individual Emperor to deal with as he saw fit. Many of the recent Emperors had chosen to ignore the spread of Christianity rather than to try and stop it, thereby causing it to flourish openly. Now monasteries and churches existed side by side with temples dedicated to the worship of pagan gods. Rome, it seemed, offered a smorgasbord of religious choices, so that who or what a person honored and worshiped had less to do with the state and more to do with personal decision than it had in previous times.

Patara had one Christian monastery, which had largely been established and funded by means of Ephanus' family coffers. The monks who lived there took vows of poverty and chastity, forsaking worldly goods and worldly pleasures, yet through loving contributions of the parishioners they lived and thrived and had no lack of the basic necessities. It was to this monastery that Ephanus and his family now made their way, laden with the morning's purchases.

The monastery stood at the edge of town, where the land sloped in gentle undulations toward the sea. The great stone structure boasted heavy oak doors and a tall, sturdy bell tower. The chapel, with its wide steps leading up to a broad portico, stood with its doors facing the public street. The rest of the edifice, containing the kitchen, dining hall, dormitories, offices, and studies, was connected to the place of worship by a series of covered passages. A network of hallways and staircases graced the interior, allowing easy access to all parts of the building. Outside, the monastic walls were surrounded by sizeable pieces of pastureland and farmland, bordered by a forest that lay between the monkish grounds and the sea, and which served as a buffer from the strong sea breezes. A rear courtyard stretched between the main buildings and the stables, which generally held some of the finest horses, cattle, sheep, pigs, and goats in the Mediterranean region. The livestock was given frequently to the monastery in the form of charitable donations from those who wished to ensure their eternal destination in an age when the very rich often believed it possible to buy one's way into Heaven. Thus, blessed by the prosperity of a number of its followers, the monastery served as an active participant in local commerce, contributing fresh eggs, dairy goods, wool, meat, and produce to the city's economy.

Architecturally, the chapel and its many connected sections followed the orderly symmetry of Roman design—its stonework walls were arranged in boxlike squares and rectangles and it had flat roofs and rectangular doorways. Atop the bell tower, which rose above the rest of the structure in the shape of a perfect square, stood a golden cross, the Christian symbol that in recent years had grown more and more prominent in cities throughout the Empire, and which represented the chosen faith of those worshiping beneath the roof over which it had been placed.

Instead of entering through the large and public chapel door Ephanus, as was usual on market days, brought his family around to the rear courtyard, which they entered through an unlocked gate in the stone wall. He led the way to a small porch with a side door, which served as the entry to both the common room and the kitchen area.

In response to his knock on the heavy oak door, a pair of

Christian brothers in black robes escorted Ephanus, Joana, and Nicolas into the common room where Abbot Stephanus joined them a moment later.

"How is my brother?" beamed the jolly voice of Stephanus, whose rotund form shook with hearty laughter, reminding Nicolas of nothing so much as the wine sloshing about in a nearly-full wineskin. "And my dear sister, Joana? And my nephew Nico?"

The two brothers could not have been a greater study in contrasts. Whereas Ephanus was lean and trim, Stephanus was large and well-fed. Whereas Ephanus had a quiet, even shy disposition and spoke in soft tones, Stephanus' voice reverberated loudly throughout any space his massive frame occupied. The elder was quietly assertive, whereas the younger, in spite of his joviality, was boldly intimidating at times. The Abbot took a stern and authoritative approach to supervising the monastery and the men in his care—his devotion to duty contrasting sharply with his normally carefree attitude. Ephanus, who held the strings to the family purses, lived simply and meagerly, while Stephanus, who had renounced all worldly goods and taken vows of poverty, appeared to live like a king, or at least to eat like one.

"We have brought another week's worth of rations," said Ephanus.

The Abbot went from bundle to sack to basket, inspecting the goods eagerly, holding up any odd pieces of fruit or loaves of bread for inspection—as though he might choose to not accept any that were less than perfect. It was clear by his size that this never happened. When finished, he laughed heartily and waved his hands for the brothers of his order to remove the goods to the larder, which they did in almost no time.

"More to give away, eh?" he chuckled, giving Nicolas a friendly nudge under the chin with his massive forefinger. "I tell you, the poor of Patara live better than . . . why, what on earth is the matter, Nico? You look as though someone you loved has died."

A tear trickled down Nicolas' cheek as his uncle scrutinized him. "What is it? You can tell Uncle Stephanus."

"He is sad because we do not live as others of our class," explained Ephanus. "He would like more of the worldly goods, and, I fear, less of the spiritual ones." Joana clicked her tongue as she, too, cast anxious eyes on her son.

"It isn't that at all," said Nicolas to Stephanus. "I just want—I just want—"

At that moment another visitor entered the room. If Nicolas' thoughts had manifested themselves in the form of a person, they could not have acted more quickly or precisely. The boy Petrus Maximus, wearing an air of confidence as fully becoming as his fine clothing, strode into the common room and bowed low to everyone assembled. Like Nicolas and his parents, the boy also carried a bundle of foodstuffs—although one much smaller.

"Greetings, Father Stephanus," said Petrus. "My mother wishes you to have these choice pickings from the marketplace to help feed the needy."

"Thank you, Master Maximus," said the Abbot.

Petrus cast an unfamiliar eye over the trio of other visitors, and directed a questioning look at Stephanus.

"This is my brother and his family," said the Abbot. "Ephanus and your father used to be the closest of friends. Here is his wife Joana, and their son, Nico . . . excuse me, Nicolas."

Petrus shook hands formally and politely.

"What is this?" asked Ephanus. "I thought your father worshiped the Roman gods. I can hardly believe he would support a ministry of the church in this way."

"If he worships anyone, my father worships Bacchus, god of wine," said Petrus, with a cynicism unusual in a boy of nearly eight. "My mother is a Christian, and it is from her that this tribute comes."

"Tribute?" protested Stephanus. "You make it sound more like an obligation than a gift."

"Helping the poor is an obligation for Christians, is it not?" asked Petrus. "We do it because it is our duty to help those less fortunate."

"And because God loves and cares for the poor as much as for the rest of us," added Ephanus, quietly but correctively.

Petrus ignored both the words and the implied admonition. He directed his attention to Nicolas. "Would you step outside with me, please? I would like a word with you."

Nicolas glanced at his mother and father, seeking permission to go with the boy he so greatly wanted to get to know. Ephanus nodded, though he did not smile or look very approving.

On the monastery steps, Petrus extended his hand once more. "Nicolas, is it? I am Petrus."

"Nico," corrected Nicolas. "Call me Nico." He looked in amazement at the waiting chariot and the magnificent horses that pulled it. Up close, they appeared even more impressive than they had from a distance.

"Very well, Nico," said Petrus, adjusting the jeweled clasp of his cloak. "I wanted to speak with you because there are very few boys my age with whom I am permitted to associate. People of our social standing, I mean. I would very much like for us to be friends."

There was an earnestness in Petrus' manner that won Nicolas over completely, yet there was also a hint of imperiousness in the black-haired boy's tone that the golden-haired boy recognized but chose to ignore. Evidently, not many people refused to honor the wishes of Petrus Maximus.

"Well?" asked Petrus.

Nicolas at first was too astonished to speak. He had been wishing for this very thing since the moment an hour earlier when he had first seen his dark-haired companion.

"Y-yes, of course," stammered Nicolas. "I just never dreamed that—"

"Next week is my birthday," said Petrus, interrupting

him. "My father is taking me to the chariot races, and I would like for you to join us."

"I would be honored, Master—"

"Petrus," said the other boy. "Just call me Petrus. Then I can count on you to accompany us, Nico?"

"By all means."

"Fine. I will tell my father. I am sure he will be pleased that I have made friends with the son of his old friend. I will bring the chariot for you at one o'clock on Wednesday. I am very happy to have met you, Nico. Good day."

With a swish of his scarlet cloak, Master Maximus descended the steps of the monastery and stepped into the chariot. When he had given instructions to the driver, the vehicle started off through the streets of Patara.

"It's time to go home," announced Ephanus, as Nicolas reentered the common room.

"Let the boy stay for a while," urged the Abbot. "I have plenty of chores he can help me with, and it will give us time to have a talk."

"Very well. Is that agreeable to you, Nico?"

The boy nodded.

Joana and Ephanus departed, while Stephanus took Nicolas into his private study. Drawing an item from his desk, he held it mysteriously in his hand as though baiting the boy to ask questions about it.

"Tell me, Nico—have you ever held all of the money in the world in your hand at one time?"

Expecting some sort of joke or trick from this most jovial of uncles, Nicolas shook his head.

"I have a purse," said Stephanus, "that never runs out of money. It is always full and always stays that way. Sounds like magic, doesn't it?"

Nicolas nodded.

"Now, we are Christians, you and I. We don't believe in magic, but in miracles. This purse in my hands is a miracle."

"Is it tied so tightly that nobody can ever get it open?" asked Nicolas, starting to laugh a little in spite of himself.

"No, but I like the way you're thinking. You knew there was a trick to it—and here it is!"

The Abbot thrust a silken purse into the boy's hand. Nicolas turned it over and over, trying to figure out which was the outside and which the inside. It had been sewn together in such a way that the inner lining stretched all around it until it became the outer surface, and the outer part turned itself around into the inner side. No matter which way he turned it, the boy could not make it come out straight. After a few moments, he cast a puzzled eye at his uncle.

"It's called a Fortunatus purse, my lad, and because its inside is its outside, and its outside is its inside, it contains all of the money in the world, and it never runs out." He took the purse into his own hands and held it up proudly. Then he put it back on the desk.

Nicolas continued to look at his uncle questioningly. He did not understand what the Abbot was trying to tell him.

"I am a poor man," said Stephanus. "Your father, being the firstborn, has all of the money in the family. When I took my vows, I pledged to live as a poor man with no possessions and to give myself to no woman. I pledged to keep my body and my life clean and pure for service to God, and I have kept those vows. I own nothing and everything I am given comes from charity. I have never married, nor do I have a devoted son like you, however, I am content that it should be so. I am happy and fulfilled in my life and could wish for no greater destiny for you than for you to follow in my path. I know that if your heart truly belongs to God, you can also find true contentment in poverty and chastity."

Nicolas' grey eyes stood fixed upon his uncle. He felt almost ashamed of the feelings he had been experiencing.

"Feeling a bit discontented, are we?" asked Stephanus.

Nicolas looked around him nervously. It was as though his uncle could read his mind.

"It's all right—we are alone. You may say what you wish."

"I—love my parents with all my heart," said Nicolas. "But they live a more austere and frugal existence in the world than you live in the monastery. I long for the finer things in life and that is something they just don't understand."

"Perhaps you are the one who doesn't understand, Nico," said Stephanus, gently. "You could have anything, and I mean anything, that your young heart desires. However, your father doesn't feel you are ready yet, and neither do I."

"Master Petrus has—"

Stephanus put up a hand. "You have just met a boy who is your own age, and has everything he wants. You feel somehow cheated out of the kind of life you should be living, and the kind of things you should be having. You have seen the moon, and now you want it for yourself."

Nicolas felt his face reddening as he looked down at the floor of the monastery.

"You have much more right now than that other boy has or ever will have. A loving father . . . a loving mother . . . and a doting uncle who looks upon you as the sort of son he would want had he chosen a different path."

Nicolas looked up. Tears filled his eyes and blurred his vision. "You are right, Uncle Stephanus. I should be content . . . but I am not."

Stephanus smiled tenderly. "Some day you will get over wanting the moon, but while you are longing, long for the things of God: love, laughter, to be a help to others. These things will last forever. Chariots get smashed, horses die, fine clothes get eaten by moths, but the love of God endures."

"I will try to remember what you have told me," said Nicolas, hugging his uncle. Stephanus' words had made him understand with his head, although discontentment still gnawed at his heart.

"Thank you for listening to the lectures of a loquacious old man," said Stephanus. "Now come with me. As I said, I have chores to do. I am going to give food to the poor and you can distribute the parcels."

The words of Stephanus played over and over again in his mind as Nicolas helped his uncle that afternoon, delivering packages of food to hungry families. In his mind he knew his uncle was right, but all the same he kept wishing and longing for the things he could not have. The more he saw of want, and hunger, and gratitude for small favors, the more he desired to escape into a life of ease and comfort.

CHAPTER THREE:

A Day at the Races

By the time Petrus' birthday arrived, Nicolas found himself in a terribly downcast state. He felt completely unworthy of the honor of accompanying the great Magistrate and his son to the chariot races. He had nothing, not one thing, to compete with the boy whose material status he so envied, and his father wasn't any help at all since he would not let Nicolas use his money for anything frivolous. "I won't have any of the finer things till I'm ninety," grumbled Nicolas, bitterly.

His spirits revived somewhat when Petrus' chariot with its sleek Arabians arrived in front of his house. The chariot was driven by a tall, clean-shaven man with dark hair and bushy eyebrows. Petrus wore an entirely new toga and cloak, and rings on his fingers, in honor of his birthday. His raiment sparkled in the spring sunshine. Nicolas felt ashamed of his own simple grey garments, but he didn't let it dampen his mood for long. He sprang eagerly into the chariot and introduced himself to the tall man.

"I'm Nicolas, son of Ephanus," he said. "It is an honor to meet you, Senator Maximus."

Petrus laughed. "This isn't my father," he said. "This is my driver."

"A pleasure to meet you, young Nicolas," said the chariot driver, his eyes twinkling with amusement as he shook the boy's hand.

"I thought your father was taking you," said Nicolas.

"So did I," said Petrus, with a faint sigh. "But my father is a very important man, and he had business to attend to that is of much more consequence than the races."

"My father is extremely busy, too," murmured Nicolas, more to himself than to his friend, "but he always has time for me. If he doesn't have the time, he makes time."

"Well, when you move in the circles my family moves in, you have to expect this kind of thing," said Petrus. "Besides, my father knew that I would have you for a companion, so he knew that I would be all right."

Never had Nicolas experienced a more thrilling after-noon. He relished the sight of the magnificent chariots as they careened around the stadium. His enjoyment was marred only by the realization that he would never have a horse or a chariot of his own, despite his father's vast wealth. It didn't seem fair — especially when the sport bred such fine athletes and horses, and made for such a grand spectacle.

After the first few minutes, Nicolas became aware that his friend was putting money on the outcome of every race. Between each event a man came to their seats and Petrus would empty more gold coins from the seemingly inexhaustible supply in his purse into the man's hand.

"You're betting on the races?" asked Nicolas, in sur-prise.

"Of course," said Petrus. "It makes the races more inter-esting that way."

"But are you allowed?"

"There is no age limit on the betting," said Petrus.

"I mean, your parents. They allow you to gamble?"

Petrus shrugged. "My mother doesn't know. And even if she did know, she understands nothing about sport. As for my father — well, he doesn't care what I do."

The last race ran just before dusk, at which time the crowd dispersed from the stadium, and Petrus took Nicolas home.

"I lost a hundred gold pieces today," observed the black-haired boy, holding his silk purse upside down and shaking it out as they rode through the streets of the town.

"Will your parents make you pay it back?" asked Nicolas, astonished that anyone his age would even be entrusted with such an amount.

"They won't notice the loss," said Petrus. "It's one of the best things about being rich—you can lose all the money you want, and it doesn't matter."

Nicolas sighed.

"What is it, Nico? Something is bothering you, I can tell. Didn't you have a good time today?"

"No . . . I mean, yes. And thank you. It's just that . . . well, my family doesn't live as well as you. Even though my father has plenty of money, he won't spend it."

Petrus' face wore a sage expression, like that of a doctor diagnosing a patient with a common illness. "Well, some people are like that—cautious, careful, thrifty. They'd rather save their fortunes than use them."

"He uses his money to feed the poor," muttered Nicolas, miserably.

"So do we all. My mother sends generous donations weekly to the monastery. You know that—that's how you and I first met."

"But your family doesn't do without like—oh, it doesn't matter, I guess."

"Do without?" asked Petrus, as though trying unsuccessfully to fit the words into his mouth. "Nico, do you mean you don't have *anything? Not anything?*"

"Nothing," said Nicolas.

"You have a horse of your own, at least," said Petrus. "There'd have to be something wrong with someone who didn't at least have a horse of his own."

"Naturally, I have a horse!" snapped Nicolas before he

had time to think about what he was saying. "Yes . . . doesn't everyone?"

Petrus nodded. "What kind is it?"

"It's . . . uh . . . white. A white mare."

"What's its name?"

"Its name? Uh, right. Its name . . . oh, mercy . . . oh . . . that's it!" Nicolas snapped his fingers. "Its name is Mercy."

"Took you long enough to remember. You haven't had the horse very long then, I take it?"

"Oh, no, it's new," said Nicolas. *Brand* new."

"I'd like to see your horse," said Petrus, decisively. "Not tonight of course, it's late. But I'll come by next week to see it. Whoa! Here's your house. Thanks for helping me celebrate my birthday, Nico."

"Happy Birthday, Petrus," said Nicolas, as he got out of the chariot.

"I'll see you next week," said Petrus.

"Yes, certainly," said Nicolas to himself as he watched the chariot depart.

He could have kicked himself for telling such a lie. Next week! Petrus would expect to see his horse next week. And he didn't have a horse. If he couldn't make good on his boast, that would be the end of it. Petrus would never speak to him or associate with him again. Returning inside, Nicolas avoided his parents and went straight to his room, where he cried himself to sleep.

CHAPTER FOUR:

One Horse

"Father," said Nicolas firmly, "I want a horse."

Ephanus stood on the balcony, gazing at the starry sky, as Joana had done on that night more than seven years earlier when the two discussed their desire for a child. Nicolas had brushed aside the curtain and now stood with his legs spread apart in a commanding position, like a young prince about to make a new proclamation.

"What is wrong with the legs God gave you, son? Can you no longer walk?"

"Poor people walk," said Nicolas. "We are not poor. People in our social standing of life ride."

"Our social standing of life?" asked Ephanus. "Since when did such things matter to you?"

"Please, Father," said Nicolas. "I must have a horse of my own. Master Petrus is only a little older than I, and he has a fine chariot, with horses to pull it. We don't even own one horse."

"One horse is a great expense," said Ephanus. "You could feed a thousand people for a week for the price of one horse. Then the horse must be fed, and a horse eats a great deal. And it must be stabled. I would much rather use the money to feed the poor than to incur such extravagant expenses."

"Still, it surely wouldn't bankrupt you to buy a horse for me. Then I wouldn't have to walk everywhere."

"No," said Ephanus. "I do not think you are ready to own a horse. Nor am I ready to buy you one. We have no room for a horse, no stable."

"There is room in the back of the house for one. It wouldn't cost all that much to build a stable for my very own horse, would it?"

"You would have to spend a lot of time feeding it and taking care of it."

"We could hire a servant to do that. I know you're rich enough to afford one more servant. Please, Father."

"Are you sure, Nico, that this is what you really, really want?"

"Oh, yes, Father. Yes! I want a horse more than anything!"

Ephanus took an appraising look at his offspring, flesh of his flesh, the child that he and his wife had so longed to have. The boy could perceive his father's disappointment as he endured the scrutiny. Nicolas had seen that look before, and it had always meant that his father would not give in. The young one's vision blurred for a moment as a tear filled his eye and trickled down his cheek. A long, bony finger reached down and gently brushed it away.

"When you were but a babe, less than one day old, you stood up and blessed God, and your mother and I took it for a sign that you would lead a holy and Christ-like life. It would seem now that our miracle child has many lessons to learn before he will be ready to fulfill his early promise."

Recollecting nothing of the miracle that he had supposedly performed at his birth, the boy neither understood nor believed that he had ever been capable of any such thing, and so dismissed it from his mind. His obsession kept his attention focused on the one object of his desire. Nicolas' heart pounded as he thought of a horse and of his lie to his friend. He could perceive from his father's tone and from the earnestness of his manner that the next moments would tell the tale of what the future would hold. He realized that if the answer was no, his father would always refuse to use his money for him for as long as both of them lived, and he would never live the kind of life he so coveted. If the answer was yes, however, he would gain the keys to a world he had, until now, only dreamed of entering.

"I believe it is the will of God that you should learn a lesson, my son," said Ephanus, solemnly.

The boy's shoulders began to droop.

"The lesson is how to handle your greatest wishes once they have come true," his father went on. "So, yes, I shall buy you a horse."

Nicolas clapped his hands and jumped up and down for joy. "Oh, thank you, Father! Thank you! I know just the kind I want . . . a white mare! And its name shall be Mercy!"

Now that the issue had been resolved for the moment, Ephanus relaxed and smiled at his son, "Why do you wish to name it Mercy? Because of God's mercy in giving it to you?"

"Partly," confessed Nicolas, "but mostly because of His mercy in not making me a liar!"

He lingered in his bed after he awoke the next morning, wondering how soon his father would take him to the market-place. Thoughts of his impending gift so filled his mind that he even thought he heard a horse whinnying. Suddenly, he realized that he hadn't imagined the sound. He jumped out of his bed, ran to his window, and flung it open. There in the courtyard stood his parents and his Uncle Stephanus. The Abbot held a rope, the other end of which dangled loosely around the neck of a snowy, white mare with a silky mane—the most beautiful horse Nicolas had ever seen.

Pausing only long enough to dress himself, the golden-haired boy darted from his room, flew out to the yard, flung his arms around each of his parents in turn, embraced his uncle, and finally reached up to stroke his—*his*—new mare.

"It is a large horse, and you are a small boy," said Stephanus, lifting Nicolas off the ground so that he could more easily stroke the mare's long, elegant head. "But you are growing fast and so it will soon be just the right size for you, I think."

Joana helped Stephanus to lift the boy onto the horse's back. As yet, it had no saddle. Nicolas, astride the back of his very own horse, felt as though he were the master of the world. His face beamed as he looked down at his uncle and his mother. "Your father went to the marketplace very early, while you remained asleep, because he wanted to surprise you with this." She smiled encouragingly at her son, trying to get him to express some gratitude.

"This is the best gift I have ever had! Thank you, Father! Thank you so very much! Why, even Petrus' Arabs aren't half as fine as this magnificent mare!"

"I hope you are not going to keep comparing yourself to Petrus," protested Ephanus, but the boy did not hear him or else chose not to pay attention, for his Uncle Stephanus was leading him around the yard, giving him pointers on riding as he struggled enthusiastically to keep his seat.

That very day, workmen arrived to build a stable. Ephanus hired a servant to act as groom, stable hand, and riding instructor, although Stephanus broke free from the monastery whenever possible to teach Nicolas from his own extensive knowledge of horsemanship. The father took his son to select a saddle—and the boy, as could have been predicted based on his recent behavior, picked out the costliest one he could find, one studded with jewels, its fringe sewn with gold thread.

Nicolas loved his horse. Even Petrus admitted that the mare Mercy was more beautiful than his own steeds. The two boys rode together frequently, once Nicolas had mastered the basics of staying in the saddle. He felt proud, riding through the city streets side by side with his black-haired companion, mounted on Mercy's back while his friend rode one of the Arabian stallions. At last it seemed to him that people would think of them as equals, that he for once looked as important and noble as the princely boy he so idolized. Nicolas felt as though his greatest wish had come true.

CHAPTER FIVE:

More Presents for Nico

"Nico, whenever we take a chariot ride, why must we always use my chariot?"

Nicolas turned pale. He had feared such a question for many months. "What do you mean, Petrus?" he asked.

"Why can we not use *your* chariot?"

"You know very well why not, Petrus. I haven't got a chariot. I was fortunate enough that my father bought me my horse."

"One horse is not enough," said Petrus, firmly. "You must have another horse. Then you could have a chariot as fine as mine."

"I don't need two horses. Mercy is strong enough to pull a chariot by herself."

"A *small* chariot, yes. But a two-horse chariot like the one I have is much bigger and more impressive. And if you had a chariot like mine, we could have races of our own."

Nicolas thought it over carefully. "I suppose it would be all right," he murmured.

"Certainly it would, Nico. Your father has plenty of money. He could buy a whole fleet of chariots and it wouldn't make a dent in his fortune. It's your birthday soon, so start asking for it right away."

"I don't know," mused Nicolas. "I had to work awfully

hard just to get him to buy the horse. I don't think he will allow me to have a second horse *and* a chariot."

"Make him promise to get you what you want. He is a Christian. He won't break his promise."

"All right," Nicolas agreed.

One afternoon, Joana had gone to the convent hospital to nurse the sick, while Ephanus remained at home going over household expenses. Nicolas approached his father, who sat at a desk with several scrolls unrolled in front of him. It was nearly time for lessons, which in Roman times were taught by fathers to their sons when those sons were as young as Nicolas. Ephanus set aside the lists of expenses and brought forth the scrolls for his son's studies.

"I usually have to summon you for lessons," said the father, gently. "What brings you so willingly today, Nico?"

"I must talk with you," said the boy, gravely and with an underlying sense of urgency.

"Very well, what do you wish to talk about?" asked Ephanus.

Nicolas cleared his throat, glanced at the floor, clenched and unclenched his fists nervously, and took a deep breath before leading up to his subject.

"Father," he said, "I'm very grateful for the mare you gave me."

"Good," said Ephanus. "I am grateful that God gave me the means to make you happy."

"In fact," Nicolas went on, "I like the mare so much that I want another."

Ephanus raised an eyebrow. "Another?"

"Yes. It will be my birthday soon, and that is what I would like for a present. There is enough room in the stable for two horses. And you wouldn't need an extra servant this time, because one man can take care of two almost as easily as he can one."

Ephanus stared long and hard at his son. Then he took

a deep breath. "Very well. You shall have two horses. Now, is there anything else you want for your birthday?"

Nicolas felt himself blushing. His father had seen right through him. "A — anything else?" he stammered, having been taken by surprise by the directness of the question.

"Yes, now that you are going to have two horses, you will want a chariot like Petrus,' will you not? Is that not what this is leading up to?"

Nicolas swallowed. "Yes, sir."

Ephanus looked his son in the eye. "Nico, you are not Petrus. You will never be Petrus. He is as different from you as the moon is from the sun. It is useless to continually want what someone else has. It will not make you happy."

"It *will* make me happy," promised Nicolas. "I know it will."

"Very well," said Ephanus. "You shall have a chariot. As fine a chariot as Petrus.' Is there anything else?"

"Yes," said Nicolas, growing bolder with the granting of each request. "If I am to ride about the town in a chariot, then I will need some fine clothes."

"Nico, the clothes you have are clean and whole. You have new clothes whenever you need them."

"Ordinary clothes. The same kind of clothes you give to the poor. I want crisp, new, brightly-colored togas and golden sandals. I want a golden circlet for my head. Oh, yes, and I also want a scarlet cloak with a jeweled clasp."

"Like the ones Petrus has."

"Yes."

The boy detected anger in his father for the first time in his life. While Ephanus' outward gaze remained cool and expressionless, Nicolas perceived that he had kindled the fires of rage inside his father. The older man may never have shown it, but Nicolas knew that his father was very, very angry with him.

Ephanus' tone of voice grew flat and nearly inaudible.

"Very well," he said at last. "You shall have *another* horse, a fine chariot, and fine clothes."

"Thank you, Father," said Nicolas, not daring to ask for anything more, even had there been anything more to ask for. He had won the victory. The things were his. Despite this, he didn't feel particularly triumphant.

He settled down to do his lessons with a lump in his throat. During the entire session, he could not bring himself to look his father in the eye.

CHAPTER SIX:

A Lesson Learned
the Hard Way

Ephanus spared no expense in his celebration of Nicolas' eighth birthday. For the first time in many years, the modest little house in a modest section of Patara rang with merriment. Musicians played lively tunes while the guests danced, played games, and sampled fine wines. The guests included many friends and relatives that Ephanus and Joana had not seen in years, chiefly the family of Senator Maximus.

Priscila sat next to Joana and boasted openly about the accomplishments of her little Petrus, while Joana, happy enough just to have a child of her own, tolerated the torrent of implied critical comparisons with a smiling face.

Sergius complimented Ephanus for letting go of the purse strings for once. "After all, no need to live like a monk all the time," he observed, lifting a goblet of wine in salute to his host and drinking it down as though it were nothing at all. "No offense, of course," he added, as he wiped his mouth with the sleeve of his tunic giving a nod to Abbot Stephanus, who stood nearby.

"None taken," murmured the old Abbot dryly.

As for Petrus, he truly seemed to savor his friend's good fortune. He constantly went out with Nicolas to the stables to

59

look at the horses and the new chariot, and constantly complimented his companion on the new, stylish-looking clothes, which included a scarlet cloak nearly identical to Petrus' own favorite garment.

During the next several months, the two boys could nearly have passed for twins, save for the golden hair of the one and the raven-black hair of the other. They became constant companions, taking turns riding in each other's chariots, going into town to make extravagant purchases, and even occasionally placing bets on the races. Only with a great deal of unease did Nicolas take part in the latter activity, for he knew his father strongly disapproved of gambling. Surprisingly though, Ephanus paid each and every debt incurred by his son, and did not punish him—unless reproving and disappointed looks could be considered punishment.

After a time, however, the continued company of a rich friend drove Nicolas to further discontentment.

"Father," he said one day, "I'm very grateful for the horse Mercy, and the other horse Charity, and for the magnificent chariot and the fine clothes, but there is something I still must have if I am to take my place among the important and wealthy people of the world."

"What is it you need, at eight years of age?" asked Ephanus, wearily.

"I need a house," said Nicolas solemnly. "I need to live in a place that is spacious and grand. The house we live in is fine for you and mother, but these are modern times, and those who truly matter in this world must live in luxury and splendor. The Emperor has a palace, and are we not even wealthier than the Emperor? I want to live in a grand and beautiful house."

"Will you never be satisfied?" asked Ephanus.

"A house, Father. Petrus' father has two fine villas in the country, and the house they live in here in Patara is three times the size of our own. Please, Father, buy me a beautiful, grand house."

Ephanus pondered this request for a few moments. "Very well," he said at length. "You shall have your house. But this time there will be certain conditions attached."

"Thank you, Father. What conditions might those be?"

"You must think over your request very carefully and ask me again in one month's time. If you still want a house of your own by then, I will buy you the largest, grandest, most magnificent house in all of Lycia. But you must not ask me again before the month is up, or I will refuse your request."

"That is fair," said Nicolas, nodding his head sagely, with all of his eight-year-old wisdom.

"During that time, I will arrange for you to live with Petrus and his family, so that you can learn what it is to lead a wealthy life."

Nicolas' grey eyes grew wide with wonder. "Oh, Father, could I? Oh, thank you! I promise to be on my best behavior the entire time I am with them."

"It is not *your* behavior that I am concerned about," said Ephanus, cryptically.

On the appointed day, Ephanus and Joana personally took Nicolas to the magnificent home of the Maximus family. Sergius and Priscila greeted them warmly, and each embraced young Nicolas in turn. "We are so glad you are allowing him to be part of our family for a little while," said Sergius to his old friend. "We will take the best care of him."

"Yes," added Priscila, her beautiful face beaming down upon the boy. "We will treat him like a prince."

Ephanus nodded, and drew a teary Joana away from her hundred and first farewell caress of that day. "Goodbye, my son," said the father, casting a final, unsmiling gaze at his offspring.

Nicolas felt frozen by his father's icy demeanor, and deep down he knew that his desires were causing grievous hurt to those who loved him. For although his father had allowed this visit (had even arranged it), in the midst of doing so Ephanus had regarded his son as though the boy had deliberately chosen to throw himself to a pack of wild wolves. This visit, and the promise of a house, did not meet with his father's approval. Nicolas realized this, and the shame that he momentarily experienced kept him awkwardly motionless in the entryway of the Maximus household. He stood contemplating whether to stay and fulfill his heart's desire with no guarantees of receiving the love and care to which he had become accustomed, or repent and flee to the safety of his own home.

Petrus broke the ice. He came forward as Nicolas' parents departed. "Welcome, Nico, welcome," he greeted, effusively. "I can hardly believe our good fortune. Now for an entire month you and I can be well and truly brothers." It was a phrase Petrus would repeat often.

As Petrus embraced his would-be brother, Ephanus and Joana lingered on the steps outside the lavish Maximus villa. The boy could not help overhearing their conversation, as perhaps Ephanus had intended.

"How can you do this, Ephanus? How can you give our son away so lightly?" asked Joana, her tone of voice sounding heartbroken.

"Just now, he is more their son than ours. I hope to cure him of being envious once and for all."

"He has already been very naughty and disobedient, and yet you have rewarded him by giving him exactly what he wants."

Ephanus laughed—a dry, bitter sort of laugh. "Reward? I hardly think so. I have given him the greatest punishment anyone could devise. He seems determined to place his head in the lion's mouth. I only hope he will learn his lesson and change his ways in time, before ending up as godless and depraved as his host."

His parents walked away but his father's words had sent a chill down Nicolas' spine. The boy knew well that Ephanus was no fool, yet punishment? How could living in luxury with his closest friend be a punishment? It made no sense, but the pointedness of his father's words lingered and kept him more wary and watchful than he might otherwise have been, and this prevented him from enjoying himself as fully as he had hoped to do.

Petrus had apparently heard nothing of the conversation, or else it mystified him so much that he at once dismissed it from his mind. The dark-haired boy showed his friend around the villa. He led Nicolas down a long corridor to a well-appointed, elegantly furnished room. The bed had silk sheets and satin pillows. Beautiful red draperies hung from the walls, and a great gilt window looked out onto an immense courtyard. "This will be your room, Nico," said Petrus. "Mine is the next one over."

Black-haired Petrus then took golden-haired Nicolas to the stables, where Nicolas' two horses, Mercy and Charity, were being looked after by highly competent stable boys. The horses, the chariot, and all of Nicolas' fine wardrobe had been sent over for his use during his stay. The boys compared the virtues of their respective horses.

"My black Arabs are the fastest horses in all of Lycia," boasted Petrus.

"My white mares are fast, too," said Nicolas.

"Very well, Nico—we shall have a race before you leave here. Fifty gold pieces says that I will win."

Nicolas' face reddened. He could not resist the implied challenge. "Why not make it a hundred gold pieces?" he asked.

"Now you've got it!" exclaimed Petrus. But before the two boys could shake hands on the deal, Petrus cried out, "*Two* hundred gold pieces!"

"A *thousand!*" laughed Nicolas, and even Petrus began to get uneasy over such a sum as that.

The black-haired boy added no more to the wager, but the two shook hands then and there, agreeing that each would put up one thousand gold pieces against the outcome of their race, and that the race would be held on the last day of Nicolas' visit.

They momentarily forgot the wager, for they were suddenly confronted by a sumptuous banquet that had been prepared in Nicolas' honor. Savory pork, roast goose, exotic fruits from far-off places, garden-fresh vegetables, and newly-baked bread made but a portion of the gargantuan feast. As they sat on couches to take their meal together as a family, Sergius spread his arms out wide. "All for you, my fine young prince," he said. At his words, servants began handing around the hot, steaming dishes. Instead of sitting around a table, as had been the custom with Nicolas and his parents, the Maximus family dined in Roman fashion. Seated on comfortable, cushioned chairs and divans with open spaces between, they partook one at a time of each of the many elegant dishes while the servants circulated about the room offering portions from a variety of platters. Finger bowls were proffered for the cleaning of greasy fingers. Wine was served to each member of the family and their guest, although Priscila limited the boys to one cupful apiece, while Sergius imbibed freely as the meal progressed.

"Shouldn't we—" blurted out Nicolas. Then he felt ashamed of himself for his outburst. After all, it was someone else's family, and they should follow their own customs.

All movement ceased. Everyone fell silent. Servants froze in place. Sergius, Priscila, and Petrus looked at their guest. Nicolas felt the color draining out of his cheeks.

"What were you going to say, my dearest?" asked Priscila, encouragingly.

"Yes, yes, speak up, my lad!" exclaimed Sergius. "If there is anything lacking that you desire, we shall supply it at once."

"It's just that . . . well . . . aren't we going to give thanks before we eat?"

Sergius threw his head back and laughed. "I should have known old Ephanus' son would be so well brought up," he stated. "Yes, my boy, we must give thanks."

Nicolas bowed his head and closed his eyes, but an instant

```

later opened them again. His father's way of giving thanks and Sergius Maximus' way of giving thanks were apparently quite different. Sergius had his arms spread and his eyes raised toward the ceiling.

"O Great Bacchus, giver of all good things, we give thanks and ask you to bless this food and use it to enrich our lives for the betterment of all!"

Petrus leaned over to whisper to his friend. "I told you my father is not a Christian. He does not worship as my mother and I do."

Nicolas did nothing more to disgrace himself during the dinner, which was capped by a dessert the boy had never tasted before—an icy cold treat served in a dish with fresh fruit. Nobody mentioned what it was called, but Nicolas hoped and prayed that it would be served again during his month's tenure.

After dinner, games were played. Sergius and Priscila led the two boys in a variety of clapping games, word games, and games played with a blindfold. They laughed together and had such a good time that Nicolas wished the evening would go on forever. *Punishment indeed!* he thought, scoffing at his father's recent words. *This is no punishment at all. These people enjoy their wealth and are still very loving and happy together.*

Nicolas decided right then and there that his father didn't know what he was talking about.

The next morning, he woke to find a servant waiting beside his bed. The servant washed the boy's face and brushed his hair, then looked the other way as the boy used the chamber pot to relieve himself. Sweet rolls and hot tea were brought in next, and Nicolas was assisted into his fine clothes without having to do so much as lift a finger. *I like this,* he thought. *I could live like this always.*

Petrus, likewise freshly cleaned, fed, and dressed by his own servant, burst into the room in high spirits. "I am going to town today to buy a new cloak," he announced.

"Do you *need* a new cloak?" asked Nicolas.
```

"No, but I *want* one," said Petrus.

While he observed many servants bustling about to perform their daily chores, Nicolas saw no sign of either Sergius or Priscila. "Shouldn't we ask your parents' permission before we go anywhere?" asked Nicolas. His own parents made a point of knowing where he was at all times.

"Father is at the Senate this morning," said Petrus matter-of-factly, "and Mother seldom rises before noon." With that, he led Nicolas out to the stables.

"Which chariot shall we take?" asked Petrus. "Mine or yours? I have it! We'll take both—each take his own! Then we shall be two young princes driving through town in our fine chariots!"

"But won't that put your servants to a lot of unnecessary trouble?" asked Nicolas. "They could more easily prepare one chariot for two of us."

Petrus laughed. "Who cares how much trouble the servants are put to? It's their job to do as they are told. If we want fifty chariots made ready at a moment's notice, they must obey."

As he rode along the streets of Patara behind Petrus in his own magnificent chariot pulled by his own beautiful steeds, and dressed in his own princely raiment, Nicolas realized that he had now become exactly what he had wanted to become nearly a year ago when he had first met Petrus. People waved at him as he passed. Never once on foot with his parents had he ever attracted so much notice. He felt important. He felt like somebody who really mattered in the grand scheme of things. How could life get any better than this? In spite of the thrill of it all, in the back of his brain there still pounded his father's ominous word *punishment.* Every time the word came back to him, he forced himself to dismiss it. *If this is punishment,* thought Nicolas, *let me be deserving of it for the rest of my life!*

In the marketplace, Petrus found a black cloak trimmed with gold thread. He threw it over his shoulders and admired his reflection in a nearby glass. "It goes well with my hair," he announced to the merchant. "I will take it. Now," he went on, turning to Nicolas, "we must find one for you."

"Me? But I don't want—I mean, I'm happy with what I already—I mean—"

"If I am getting a new cloak, then you surely must get one, too," insisted Petrus. "Now, yours should be gold, to match your bright golden hair." He critically examined the other cloaks.

Despite Nicolas' protests, Petrus insisted that his friend should buy a cloak at least as grand as his own, and finally they found one—a bright, golden cloak with black trim. "There!" exclaimed Petrus after the cloak had been placed around Nicolas' shoulders, and he once again employed his pet phrase. "Now we are well and truly brothers!"

Once he saw how well the new cloak suited him, Nicolas decided that perhaps his father would be willing to pay for yet another present. He agreed then and there to purchase the cloak, and the merchant agreed to forward the bill. Nicolas gave the merchant his present address rather than that of his parents' house, for he did not want it to be known how shabbily he normally lived.

After feasting at an inn that catered only to the best clientele, and leaving another large account to be forwarded for payment, the two boys got into their chariots and returned home.

This pattern went on every day for nearly the first two weeks of Nicolas' visit. Every day Petrus would desire some new thing, and then he and Nicolas would go out and get it. Though the process never seemed to bore Petrus, Nicolas found it tiresome by about the ninth or tenth day. He himself had accumulated in that time more clothing and jewelry than he could ever wear, and had spent enough money to send even an average man of wealth into bankruptcy. Still, the process of high living and extravagant spending went on. It became so tedious to Nicolas that he began to wonder if his father hadn't been right after all in calling this kind of life a punishment.

The two boys never saw Petrus' parents any more than in passing after that first night. As Nicolas came to realize, that night had been a show put on for him to make him think they were a loving, close family. He now found the opposite to be true. Whereas Ephanus seldom left the side of Joana for more than a few hours at a stretch, Sergius and Priscila appeared rarely to speak to one another. The two of them were seldom present in the villa at the same time. Sergius spent long hours on his magisterial duties, or so he claimed. Priscila paid endless visits to her women friends, or so she too, claimed. And Petrus seemed scarcely to exist for them at all. More often than not, they ignored their son completely. If Sergius ever taught Petrus his lessons, Nicolas never observed him to do so. The Magistrate scarcely seemed to spend any time at home.

Therefore, it took both boys by surprise when they arrived home early one evening from a particularly extravagant day of spending to be informed by a servant that Petrus' father wished to see them. The servant escorted them, rather forcibly, into the bath, where Sergius often went to relax upon his arrival home.

Sergius sat immersed in the hot water of the pool with his elbows resting against the tiled edge. Hot vapors of steam rose up from the water and filled the room with a misty, hot dampness. Both boys felt themselves growing warm and perspiring, having come into the room fully clad, but Sergius did not invite them to join him in his bath. Instead he gave a wave, and the servants who had been attending him departed.

"I have just been visited by merchants from the marketplace," he said, looking sternly at both his son and his son's companion. The vapors from the pool could not mask the stench of his breath. It appeared to Nicolas that his host had been drinking, and quite heavily. "It seems you two young rascals have been running up quite a pile of bills. Did either of you have a plan for how you were going to pay for all of your worthless purchases?"

Petrus swallowed hard. "I—I thought you would pay for them, sir. You always have."

"So, you feel my money is yours to throw away, is that it? And you," asked Sergius, turning to Nicolas "—who do you expect to pay for *your* extravagances?"

Nicolas glared angrily at Petrus before replying. "I—I had thought my own father would take care of it, sir," he said.

His host's tone grew gentler, but only slightly. "You are my guest, living under my roof. I consider you as much my responsibility as if you were my own son. I would not expect my oldest and best friend to pay your expenses while you are staying in my home. I intend to cover them, and to tell your father nothing about this. Now, if you had known that I, and not your father, was going to pay your bills, would you have run up so many charges?"

"N-no, sir," stammered Nicolas.

"You boys have both been very foolish," said Sergius. "There is no such thing as a bottomless well, and it is time you understood that. I am going to make sure that you both remember this from now on. I am going to teach you a lesson you will never forget."

He clapped his hands, and the servants reappeared, helping him out of the pool, drying him with towels, and dressing him in his finery. Then he ushered the boys into a room bare of furniture, having only one door and one solitary candle burning. "This is where you will stay now," announced Sergius. "You will not be allowed to use your chariots or wear any more clothes than you are wearing this minute. You will not be allowed to leave this villa without my permission. Your meals will be simple and basic. You will be allowed one hour a day to exercise in the courtyard."

"F-for how long, sir?" asked Petrus, meekly.

"Until I say differently," snarled Sergius. "Now, before I leave you in your new quarters, I have one more thing to show you."

He brought them into another room with a series of large posts stuck into the floor at intervals, and black whips and switches lining the walls. In response to his silent command, two servants removed the boys' tunics, and with leather thongs tied each by the hands to a whipping post, leaving their bare backs exposed. A servant placed a switch in his master's hand, and then the two attendants withdrew.

"I keep this room for servants who misbehave," explained Sergius. "But it serves for disciplining misbehaving boys as well." He removed his tunic, and threw it into a corner of the room. Then he raised the switch.

No, thought Nicolas. *No, this can't be happening. Not to me. Not to my princely young friend.* He said nothing, though he could feel the perspiration running down his brow.

Though clearly intoxicated, Sergius Maximus had reached the stage of fighting drunk, where his coordination had not yet been impaired to the point of being rendered unable to strike a firm, accurate blow. Frequent immersion in alcohol had accustomed his brain, in some respects, to allow him to retain mastery of his movements long after sober reason had fled.

He brought the switch down firmly upon his son's back, drawing blood on the first blow. Then he did the same to Nicolas. Again and again he raised the switch and brought it down, striking each time with powerful force.

Petrus howled loudly at each application of the switch, but Nicolas resolved to bear his pain as manfully as he could. He kept silent, though each blow brought him agony. Ten times apiece did Sergius strike, first one and then the other.

"Does your father do this often?" Nicolas managed to ask, after about the seventh blow.

"Ow! Ow! Ow!" shrieked Petrus, tears streaming down his cheeks. "As—Ow! As often as he—ow! wants!"

It seemed a relief to be locked in the bare room, bloody backs and all. Nicolas, who had felt the sting as badly as his friend but had managed not to break down, now comforted his sobbing companion.

"I had hoped something like this wouldn't happen while you were here," blubbered Petrus.

"Then why did you insist on spending so much money?" asked Nicolas.

"He's never minded about the money before," sobbed Petrus. "This is a new excuse."

"Excuse for what?"

"He's often coming up with some reason or other to beat me."

"Well, I don't think it's right. My father would never approve."

"Are you going to tell him?"

"I can't. Then your father will tell him about the debt. That's why he's paying my share of the expenses . . . to keep my mouth shut. Even when he's—well, not in his right mind—your father is still a shrewd politician."

"What would your father do if he knew about your debts? Beat you?"

"No . . . my father has never laid a hand on me, except to show affection," said Nicolas. "I just don't want him to know about the merchants' bills. I've brought enough disgrace on him, I see that now. When I can, I intend to repay the money to your father."

"Ephanus never beats you? I wish I could have a father like that."

"Up till now, I envied you for the kind of father that I thought you had. I guess nobody's parents are perfect."

Not a bed, not a chair adorned the room. The boys had to sit on the floor and lie down upon it to go to sleep, using their cloaks as blankets, since the only luxuries they had been allowed were their clothes. The solitary candle that gave the room its only light continued to burn until it burned itself out, and then they found themselves in utter darkness. Save for a few small holes for ventilation, there were no windows or other openings besides the door, so there was nothing to relieve the monotony of the dark.

Petrus lay face downward—both boys were too bruised to lie on their backs—and whimpered as he tried to go to sleep. After nearly an hour of this, Nicolas finally protested.

"Can't you shut up? Stop being such a crybaby! If he does this to you often, you should be used to it by now! I'm in as much pain as you are, and I'm not crying about it! Try to grow up! Try to be a man about it!"

"How dare you? How dare you?" Petrus had sat up in the darkness, and clearly felt stung by Nicolas' words. He jumped toward where he thought Nicolas lay, and seized him by the hair.

"Oh, don't get worked up about it," chided Nicolas. He grabbed his friend firmly by the shoulders and held on until the fight went out of the other boy. Petrus released his hold on Nicolas' hair. "I'm sorry, Petrus. I didn't mean to be unkind. Just try to go to sleep without the sobbing."

Subdued, Petrus sank back into his corner without another word, and in a few minutes his regular breathing told Nicolas that his rich friend was asleep. Nicolas mused. In their relationship, Petrus had always been the strong one, the assured one. Now the tables had suddenly turned, and it was Nicolas' strength on which Petrus relied. Nicolas didn't feel daunted or discouraged by this episode. He felt, if anything, stronger for having experienced it. He also realized that life for Petrus was not the perfect idyll he had imagined. Nicolas had wanted the moon, as Uncle Stephanus had put it, only to find it was made of nothing more than light and air.

Now Nicolas realized what his father had meant about the punishment. Yes, sending him to this house had been a form of punishment, and now that the true nature of Sergius Maximus had been exposed to him, the boy saw that Ephanus had been right after all. Not only was the Maximus family *not* a Christian family, it was not a happy family. This was the part of the lesson that Ephanus had intended him to learn. Nicolas at once knew better than to blame his father for having sent him into this den of misery. It had been done at his, Nicolas,' own urging and bidding. The beating he had just received was not part of the "punishment" his father had intended him to experience; Nicolas knew his father well enough to know that. If Ephanus had thought for one minute that the trials his son might encounter in the Maximus household would include such savagery, he would never have allowed the visit to take place. Nicolas knew he had only himself to blame. He had, as Ephanus had put it, willfully stuck his head into the lion's mouth. Should he therefore be so shocked, he asked himself, at having been bitten?

He also finally understood what his father, Uncle Stephanus, and even Sergius in his cruel way had been trying to teach him. Every good thing came with a price. Someone had to pay that price, sooner or later. Nobody could get away without paying at some point. He had tried to take, and take, and take, without ever reckoning with the fact that the money really belonged to his father and not to him at all. Suddenly, his father's objections to unnecessary expenses made sense to him. Even if one could afford it, one still had to pay for it, and money paid out was money that never came back. No wonder Ephanus had chosen, instead of merely throwing it away, to use his money to do God's work. And that Stephanus had chosen to live poor and serve God. Both men knew about paying the price. Even Sergius knew about it, although his ways of handling it were not quite as civilized.

And then it occurred to Nicolas that even Jesus, the Christ, had understood about the price. He had paid it with His own life, that mankind might know salvation and learn the way to Heaven. At that moment, for the first time in his life, Nicolas felt a glimmer of an understanding of Jesus' love, about which his parents had tried to teach him from his earliest days. With this glimmer of understanding came a feeling of reverence and closeness to God. He felt the nearness of the Savior's presence, even there in utter darkness, and knew that he was not alone, nor ever would be.

Never before had he prayed from his own heart and with his own mind. He had been taught many, many prayers by his devoted parents, but all of them he had learned to recite by rote. Now he prayed the first, true, earnest prayer of his young life.

Jesus, help me to learn the lesson my father wants to teach me. Help it to make me a better son to him. Help me to give back the love that he has always shown to me.

A tear ran down his cheek, this time not the tear of a spoiled child wanting to have what he did not need, but the tear of one who had begun to understand what love and giving were all about.

He sniffed a few times, wiped his eyes, and then settled down to rest, as a sudden urge to sleep had come upon him. Within moments he slept, deeply and dreamlessly.

CHAPTER SEVEN:

Nico Repents

Since the candle had burnt out, the two boys remained in absolute darkness. When Nicolas awoke, he heard Petrus stirring nearby, but neither boy spoke a further word. It seemed they had nothing more to say to each other. They could commiserate over their fate as fellow-prisoners, or they could make plans for what they would do when they got out. Or they could remain silent. Nicolas had enough thoughts of his own to occupy him for weeks.

As it turned out, their ordeal did not go on for weeks, or even days. It did not extend much beyond that one night.

When he heard the bolt being removed, Nicolas at once grew apprehensive. Doubtless Petrus felt the same way, as an audible gasp escaped from his throat at the sound. Was Sergius returning to inflict more punishment? A moment later, the light of day flooded the room, and both boys had to cover their eyes until their vision could adjust to the brightness. As he rubbed his eyes and looked, it appeared to Nicolas that a bevy of angels had come to minister to them. A dark maternal hand caressed his head. A pair of loving arms then wrapped themselves around him. He at first didn't know what was happening, but it felt good to be in someone's warm embrace.

By the time his dazed brain had caught up with his senses, Nicolas realized that Priscila had caught up both himself and Petrus and drawn them close to her. Her maids stood respectfully behind her.

"Oh, my poor darlings!" she cooed. "I am so sorry you were put through such an agonizing punishment." Her eyes narrowed momentarily, as an angry look flashed across them. "My husband is a brute sometimes—a savage animal. Especially when he has been drinking. Come out into the light now, and I will take care of you."

Both boys approached the hallway with caution, looking first one way and then the next, like frightened animals. "There is nothing to fear. He is gone to the law courts, and won't be home until much later," said Priscila. Her beautiful face had tears in it as she gave them tender, loving looks.

"Will we have to go back in there, before he comes home?" asked Nicolas, warily.

"No, no! I will not allow it! I did not know of this, or I would have come for you sooner. It is a disgrace that he should punish his own son in the same manner one would punish a servant! He is not a Christian, you see, and he knows nothing of mercy or compassion."

They had not mentioned Sergius by name. It was as though saying his name aloud would bring back the horrors of the night before.

Nicolas felt a little self-conscious about appearing bare-chested in front of all of these ladies, especially as he knew his back had to be a scratched and bloody mess, but under the circumstances it could not be helped. He didn't want to retrieve his cloak and tunic from the dark room.

Petrus sobbed and sobbed in his mother's arms, and appeared to have no shame about either his appearance or his childish blubbering. His mother comforted him until the sobs had been reduced to occasional gasps for breath from the exertion of all that crying.

The maids, at their mistress' bidding, anointed the boys' bruised and scarred backs with healing creams and ointments.

The fresh, fragrant scents and the soothing coolness of the applications brought almost immediate relief to Nicolas' wounds.

The next several hours passed as blissfully as the night before had passed agonizingly. Nicolas felt as though he had been transported from the depths of Hell to the heights of Heaven. Priscila had fresh clothing brought for the boys, which the maids helped them to put on, and she personally conducted them to the dining room for a sumptuous breakfast that was doubly gratifying to empty stomachs.

Petrus' mother had not shown them this much attention since Nicolas' arrival, and the latter had begun to wonder how motherly she really was. Now he had no doubt that this Christian lady, selfish though she may have appeared at times, loved her son as though he were the most precious thing on earth, just as Nicolas now realized his own mother loved him. The good woman talked with the boys and told them stories to cheer them up, remaining at the table with them until the last bite had been eaten. After the meal, she personally supervised the preparation of their rooms, and insisted that both of them go to bed at once—a mandate that neither one found it hard to comply with.

Restored to his former room with all of its elegance, Nicolas felt less dazzled by the splendor than he had ever felt before. In fact, for the first time in his short life, he wouldn't have minded a straw pallet with a burlap sack for a blanket. Before slipping between the silk sheets and drifting off to sleep on the soft pillow stuffed with feathers, Nicolas knelt and prayed a prayer of thanks for their deliverance.

The ensuing days brought a speedy lessening of the boys' wounds, as their young bodies healed quickly. Just as rapidly, Petrus resumed his former demeanor, and soon had grown as arrogant as before. He never referred to the incident of the beatings and the dark room, and he appeared to have put it out of his mind completely.

After his profound experience with the prayer, Nicolas could not so easily forget. He felt differently now toward Petrus and his family, and he longed to return to his mother and father. At first, he had resolved to return home as soon as his wounds had healed. No longer did he desire a grand house of his own, and that had been the original reason for his visit with the Maximus family. In fact, he slowly realized that he no longer wanted or needed any of the expensive luxuries he had been demanding. He resolved that the moment he arrived home, he would give back the chariot, the horses, and the fine clothes to his father, so that Ephanus could sell them or give them to the poor.

However, as the days passed, and he remained in the company and under the roof of his black-haired friend, a remnant of the old desires still flickered occasionally. It was hard to remember for long about God in a household where Bacchus was the chief idol of worship. And it was difficult to maintain a heart of compassion for the poor when a feast awaited one at every meal and the beds were so soft and comfortable.

Sergius seldom appeared in these days, and when he did, he ignored the boys. He seemed to have forgotten entirely about the extravagant expenditures, or the beatings, or any other part of that terrible night. Priscila, who now made it a point to spend more time with her son and his companion, assured Nicolas that Senator Maximus had long since forgotten all about the incident. Nicolas wondered if his friend's father had, after all, paid the bills that were owed, but he dared not ask and risk awakening the paternal wrath all over again. Still, his resolve to repay the money he owed remained strong in his heart.

When only nine days remained of the term of his visit, Nicolas learned from a servant that his parents would dine at the Maximus table that very night. The boy guessed, and probably accurately, that Ephanus wanted to see for himself how the lesson was progressing, and to gauge whether or not the extravagances would be likely to continue once his boy had returned to the shelter of his own roof.

Sergius and Priscila presented themselves as the very model of a happily married couple as they graciously welcomed their old friends to their home. Petrus, too, gave the appearance of a devoted, though somewhat spoiled son. Nicolas said nothing and did nothing to draw attention to himself throughout the entire evening.

Seated across the table from him, Joana cast loving looks in Nicolas' direction during the dinner. All he could manage to give her in return was a shy smile. His father he did not even dare to look in the eye. He felt so ashamed of his former demands, and of his arrogant attitude, that he feared he would burst into tears at any moment.

The only time Ephanus addressed his son directly was to ask, "And how is my son enjoying his treatment in this fine household?" Even then, Nicolas could find no words — at least, none that he could say in the company of his friend and his friend's family. So he nodded to his father, and looked down at his plate. He could feel his cheeks growing hot and red.

Naturally, no mention was made of the horrendous night of the beatings, nor of the expenditures the boys had made. Nicolas would not have said anything about it publicly, even had there been a risk of another like punishment for his silence. He had no desire to betray the inner secrets of his temporary family's dysfunctionality, either for the sake of Petrus or for himself.

Finding himself struck dumb in the presence of his parents had come as a surprise to Nicolas, who had at least expected to be able to conduct himself in a pleasant, sociable way. Try as he might though, he could think of nothing to say. Embarrassment about the way he had been treating his parents coupled with the embarrassment he now felt about continuing with the charade of acting like a spoiled rich boy combined to make him unable to utter so much as a good night.

He accepted his parents' farewell embraces at the end of the evening, and nodded silently as they in turn affirmed their love for him. Sergius and Priscila acted the part of the pleasant host and hostess until their friends had gone. Then they went off in separate directions, leaving the servants to escort the two boys to their beds.

The next morning, Nicolas knew what he had to do. "I am going home," he announced to Petrus and Priscila at breakfast.

Petrus gasped. "The time isn't up yet!" he exclaimed. "If you go home now, your father will never buy you the grand and beautiful new house you wanted."

"I don't want it anymore," confessed Nicolas. "I realized last night that I miss my parents too much. I want to return home to be with them."

"Let Nico go if he wants to, Petrus," said Priscila, soothingly. "It is very touching that he misses his mother and father. If my little darling Petrus were to stay with friends for a time, it would be my greatest hope that he would want to return to his loving mama." She reached over and stroked his black hair with her slim, dark hand.

"Of course I would, mama," cooed Petrus in a voice that sounded about five years younger than his age.

"When will you be leaving us?" asked Priscila, turning to her guest but still stroking her own child.

"Today . . . right now," said Nicolas.

"No, Nico!" exclaimed Petrus, in whiny, three-year-old tones. "Stay until tomorrow," he urged. "Please, please, please."

Nicolas took a deep breath. "All right," he agreed. "I'll leave tomorrow." He turned to Priscila. "I would appreciate it if you could have the servants get my things ready by then."

"Of course," said Priscila.

During the rest of that day, Nicolas and Petrus helped Priscila prepare her weekly contribution to the poor. At Priscila's insistence, all three rode in Petrus' chariot. They took their bundles directly to the monastery. As had happened the night before, Nicolas found himself tongue-tied in his uncle's presence. Abbot Stephanus gazed curiously at his nephew, but spoke no word directly to him, giving most of his attention to Priscila and her son.

That evening, Nicolas sought out Sergius, who sat in the small room where he studied his scrolls relating to matters of state. The golden-haired boy coughed politely when his knock at the open door had been ignored. Sergius looked up. "Come in, Nico," he said, welcomingly.

Trembling with fear, Nicolas strode purposefully toward the man who had punished him so severely.

Sergius' smile showed no sign of recollection of anything other than pleasant moments between them. "Yes? What can I do for you, Nico?"

Fearing the worst as a result, yet resolved to do what he had to do, Nicolas spoke up. "I—I wanted to know, sir, what you have done about the money." Beads of sweat formed on his brow as he uttered the words. He feared a torrent of anger would erupt at any moment.

His host looked at him blankly. "The money?" he asked, as though trying hard to recall what the reference could mean, and unable to come up with an answer.

"Yes," went on Nicolas. "The money. The money that Petrus and—I mean, sir, the money that I spent so foolishly in the marketplace and elsewhere. You had said you were going to pay it."

"Of course," said Sergius, vaguely, as though he still only barely remembered the matter. "What of it?"

Nicolas swallowed hard. "Well, did you? Pay it, I mean, sir."

A kindly, benevolent smile lit up the Magistrate's face. "Why, certainly I paid it, Nico. I said I would take responsibility for you while you are under my roof, and I meant it."

"Th—th—thank you, sir," stammered Nicolas. "I'm very grateful. I will pay the money back to you . . . every penny. I promise."

"It isn't necessary," said Sergius, still smiling pleasantly. "Any son of my friend Ephanus is a son of mine."

You proved that when you beat both of us till our backs bled, thought Nicolas. *And you beat your own son like that frequently, from what Petrus has told me. I am glad, glad, glad that I am not your son.* Aloud, he said, "I must repay it, sir. My father would not wish me to take such a vast sum from you, and I believe it would be the right thing to do."

"Very well, Nico, and thank you," said Sergius. "I think you meant that sincerely. You may pay the money back if you choose, of course, but there is no hurry about it. I appreciate the gesture, because it shows that you have character and morals."

Nicolas wasn't ready to retreat yet. He had one more matter to mention, knowing full well the risk involved. "I—I hope you're not still angry with me for my foolish spending. I hope you can forgive me, sir, for incurring such wasteful expenses."

Now he had lit the fuse. Surely, an explosion would result this time.

But Sergius only smiled. "Angry? I was never angry with you, Nico." He honestly seemed to have no memory of that terrible night. "How could I be angry with you? You are a fine boy. It has been a pleasure having you in my home." He reached out his large hand and shook the boy's small one.

As he left the room, Nicolas reflected on the change in Sergius. One night a raging tiger, tonight a benevolent dove. *It must be frightening not to know what kind of person your father will be from day to day,* he thought.

Later, in Nicolas' room, after the rest of the household had gone to bed, Petrus paid his friend a visit to confront him. "You can't leave yet," he informed Nicolas, in his usual swaggering tone of voice.

"Why not?" asked Nicolas, who had been trying to decide which of his clothes to keep and which to give away. He finally decided to give everything away, and go back to the simple cloth tunics he used to wear.

"Because," said Petrus, "we haven't had our race yet—our chariot race. Remember?"

"Oh, that," said Nicolas, dismissing it with a wave of his hand. "I don't want to race anymore. I concede. You win."

"That's not very sporting," chided Petrus. "Besides, we have a wager on it. A thousand gold pieces. Had you forgotten, Nico?"

"No," murmured Nicolas, "but I hoped you had."

"We're going to have the race," stated Petrus, firmly. "And one of us will be richer by a thousand gold pieces."

"All right," said Nicolas, reluctantly. "It will be the last thing I do with my chariot and my horses."

Petrus knew of a wide country lane outside the town where there would be plenty of room for two chariots. He outlined the route in a brief sketch made with a piece of charcoal on a scrap of parchment. They would race along the lane, a back road that started a little distance from Patara and curved around toward the Mediterranean, keeping its distance from the populated areas as it wound through farmlands and low hill country. "First one to reach the sea wins the thousand gold pieces," declared Petrus.

Nicolas couldn't help sharing in Petrus' enthusiasm. Although his whole heart was no longer in the race, his friend took so much delight in the prospect that Nicolas found himself caught up in the other boy's anticipation. Even though he had told himself he would not fall prey to Petrus' charms again, he found his companion too irresistible to ignore. Perhaps, after all, he thought fleetingly, despite his previous repentance, he might stay out the whole visit with Petrus and earn the fine, big mansion that he had once desired with all his heart. However, on recollection of his encounter in the dark room, he knew that he had greater things to live for, and decided that the race would represent his last experience of the extravagant life.

CHAPTER EIGHT:

The Crossroads

"He's *my* puppy!"

"No, he's not! He's *mine!*"

There never seemed to be enough of anything to go around. At dinner, Angelina had eaten the last tart, instead of dividing it into three equal pieces. Angelina had likewise taken the gold piece sent by their father, and claimed it as her own since it was "her right as the eldest." And now she tried to snatch the puppy away from Abigail, using the same reason as an excuse for petting it first.

"The puppy is *mine!* Papa's note said it belonged to *me!*" screamed Abigail.

Four-year-old Ana spoke up. "He belongs to all of us," she said, firmly.

"Give it here!" shouted Angelina, tearing the dog out of her sister's arms.

Ana trotted toward the eldest sister as fast as her short little legs could take her. Without a word, she stretched out her arms imperiously toward Angelina, as though demanding the puppy be placed there. Almost as if under a spell, Angelina lifted the dog into her youngest sister's arms.

Ana carried the puppy to Abigail, and held out its little body toward the middle sister. Abigail gratefully and somewhat humbly accepted the pet and stroked it gently. Then Ana took the puppy and presented it to Angelina, who likewise held it and caressed it.

"You can take turns," said the little one, brightly, and the two older sisters looked at each other apologetically, both ashamed that they had not thought of so simple a solution.

Aunt Marla came out of the villa. "What is all the fuss about?" she started to shout, then stopped when she beheld the peaceful scene of the three girls handing the dog around to each other. "Oh. You're all right, then," she observed.

Ever since the three girls had been thrust into her care, Marla had felt that they would be the death of her. To avoid a terrible plague which had begun to take its course through the city of Patara, their mother and father, the nobleman Florus Dorius and his wife Anabel, had sent the girls to their aunt's country villa for safety. From time to time, gifts were sent for the girls' enjoyment and as a reminder that their parents thought of them often. The tarts had been one such gift; the gold coin another. Their most recent present had been the little puppy, a white wolfhound with floppy ears, with whom all three girls had fallen in love.

The puppy pricked up its ears and gave a bark, then leaped out of Angelina's hands and ran toward the low stone fence that surrounded Marla's property. Giving a mighty bound for one so small, the puppy jumped over the fence and started running down the hill.

Angelina, who at age nine had the longest legs and could run the fastest, jumped to her feet and followed after the dog, calling "Boris! Boris!" She cleared the fence with one leap. It took the two younger girls longer to scramble over the fence, but they soon went after their sister. Aunt Marla, who had neither the agility nor the inclination to clamber over the stone structure, stood calling to them from the yard.

"Girls! Girls!"

Angelina, who had caught up to the puppy, grabbed him and held onto him tightly as though afraid he would try to run away again. "Woof! Woof!" barked the animal, wagging its tail and looking toward the valley.

Ana, catching up with Abigail, was the first to follow the puppy's gaze, and she soon spotted what had apparently excited their pet.

Aunt Marla's estate stood just beyond the port city of Patara. To the south stretched the vast waters of the Mediterranean Sea. To the east lay a wide highway that looped around the perimeter of the city. Small farms dotted the hilly terrain, each with a little path or road connecting it to the main highway, like tributaries feeding into a great river. Not far from the point where the road headed directly down to the sea, another thoroughfare crossed its path, one often used by farmers for driving their sheep or cattle to market. Nearby rose a six-foot stone wall that fenced in an orchard of cherry trees. The spot just before the road dipped down toward the water could be seen clearly from the villa.

"Look!" cried Ana. "What is that?" She pointed and the other girls followed with their eyes the direction of her finger.

Two tiny clouds of dust arose from the horizon, where the road met the eastern sky. From the east came two black dots, now one in front, now the other. Then came to the girls' ears the sounds the dog had already noticed—the sound of whips cracking and the thunderous pounding of hoof beats.

"What is it?" asked Abigail.

"Horses," murmured Ana, staring at the curious sight with awe.

"Yes," said Angelina. "And they are coming closer!" Standing up and shading her eyes from the morning sun, she gave the puppy to Ana to hold.

"Are they runaways, do you suppose?" asked Abigail.

Now it could be seen that the hoof beats were caused by two teams of horses pulling two chariots. The riders could not be distinguished, their forms being too small to be seen from such a distance.

"What is it, girls?" called Aunt Marla. "What do you see?"

"Two chariots," called back Angelina. "One has a team of white horses, while the other has a team of black."

"Runaway chariots!" exclaimed Abigail. "Oh, I hope they don't come too close!"

"I don't think they're runaways," observed Angelina. "One of the drivers is using a whip. Why, I believe they're in a race!"

"They're coming closer. I can see the drivers now," reported Abigail. "I think you're right, Angelina. They *are* racing! Why, they're only a pair of little boys, not any older than we are!"

"Yes," said Angelina. "The boy driving the white horses has golden hair, while the one driving the black team has black hair."

"Both are wearing beautiful scarlet cloaks," said Abigail. "And circlets of gold on their heads."

"I think the white team is going to win," said Angelina.

"No, I expect it will be the black team," said Abigail. "It's in the lead right now, and see how the driver cracks the whip so furiously!"

The puppy's ears pricked up at a new sound, and he barked afresh. "Boris hears something else," said little Ana. "I think it sounds like sheep."

* * * * * *

Enu the sheep farmer knew his work. He had been doing it for more than twenty years. His was the largest and the finest sheep farm on the west coast of Lycia. He especially relished market days, for on these days he took the fattest and biggest of all his sheep and drove them into town, where he commanded top prices. Butchers, meat vendors, wool dealers, servants from large houses, and even other farmers would pay dearly for even one sheep from Enu's farm. And today Enu was bringing two hundred sheep to market. He and his men prodded any of the animals that strayed, but the majority followed the rest of the flock, and so caused no trouble for the drovers, whose only task was to see to it that the sheep made it safely to the marketplace.

To their right stood a six-foot stone fence that walled in a cherry tree orchard. The sturdy wall made an "L" shape at the crossroads, where it turned sharply and ran due east for several miles. Thus the sheep were hidden from view until they emerged onto the open highway. Enu always chuckled at the impatience of any horseback riders or drivers of carts and wagons who happened to be passing on the main highway as they chafed while waiting for hundreds of sheep to make the crossing. Enu always saw to it that his sheep had the right-of-way. He didn't care if the Emperor of Rome got stuck in the traffic, as long as his sheep made it to market in time.

For twenty years, Enu had been taking his sheep to market. By this time he could have done it in his sleep . . .

* * * * * *

"I don't see any sheep," said Angelina.

"But I hear them!" cried little Ana. "Lots and lots of them! The puppy hears them, too! They sound awfully close."

"But not as close as the chariots!" exclaimed Abigail. "Look! The golden-haired boy is in the lead now!"

* * * * * *

Petrus could not help muttering some choice curses under his breath, words he had heard his father use in moments of supreme irritation. He had cracked his whip repeatedly, and still Nicolas' team was passing him. He wanted to win fairly, that was sure. So he urged his horses to greater and greater speed, faster than he had ever driven his chariot before.

Of course, he knew he would win. He had sent some of his servants to the finishing point to act as judges, and he had already bribed them to judge in his favor, regardless of the true outcome. He didn't like to cheat his best friend, but he simply could not afford to lose any more wagers, and would rather betray a dozen friendships than risk another beating. The words of his personal servants would carry more weight than those of a guest in his home whose parents lived like paupers. He knew the thousand gold pieces were as good as his, but he wanted more than anything to finish as the true winner. He cracked the whip again, and again, and again.

* * * * * *

Nicolas had never driven his chariot so fast. In truth, he had never driven it by himself before. His driver had always accompanied him, even though he often had taken the reins himself to learn how to do it. Barely able to see over the top of the front rim of the chariot, he didn't have any idea what he was doing, and he only hoped that the horses did. He held firmly onto the reins and prayed for a swift conclusion to the race, while the countryside flew by so swiftly it became a blur.

* * * * * *

"Look! Look!" cried Ana. "There are the sheep—coming out onto the crossroads. We couldn't see them before, because they were blocked from our view by that fence."

"The black team is overtaking the white team," said Abigail.

"But the white team is still ahead," said Angelina. "He's going so fast, I think he's going to win."

"No, I still think it will be the black team," declared Abigail.

"What will happen when they reach the crossroads?" cried Ana. "It's full of hundreds of sheep now!"

The puppy in her arms whimpered.

* * * * * *

The sound of pounding hoof beats reached Enu's ears long before the first sheep arrived at the crossroads. He knew that a rider or riders approached at top speed. Well, he chuckled grimly to himself, top speed or no, his sheep took priority when it came to crossing. The horsemen would simply have to stop and wait their turn. This was the way it was done. He had never stopped his sheep to accommodate a horseman or a driver, and he wasn't about to start now. Besides, once they had started across, there could be no stopping. If he separated the main herd from their leader, confusion and chaos would follow, despite all of the prodding of his men. No, the horsemen would have to wait. Any thought of doing otherwise never occurred to Enu.

He herded the sheep across the highway, while his men used their prods to keep the animals on the road to town.

* * * * * *

Unaccustomed to such a breakneck pace, Nicolas could barely see ahead of the noses of his two white horses. Everything rushed by so quickly that his eyes could scarcely adjust. By the time he had focused on a bordering rock, fence, or tree, he had already whizzed past it.

But now he saw something in his path, and there was no way to avoid it. Sheep. Hundreds and hundreds of sheep in the road. They hadn't been there a moment before, he felt certain. Had he been riding a horse alone, the animal might possibly have managed to jump over the sea of wooly creatures, but two horses pulling a chariot could never make such a leap. He could not turn right, because Petrus' chariot was close behind him on that side. He could not turn left, because a huge stone wall ran parallel to the road.

The herd lay directly in his path, and the horses plunged forward. He could not stop them quickly enough to avoid a messy collision.

What could he do?

* * * * * *

Petrus likewise saw the sheep ahead, and all at once his brain froze. Years of training, years of practice at driving his horses in his chariot, had not prepared him for this. He had no idea what to do.

Faster and faster ran his horses. He couldn't remember how to slow them. He couldn't remember anything. Not anything at all. He could only see that a catastrophe lay ahead. Preventing it or lessening the impact in any way had become impossible. The chariot continued its mad rush forward.

He dropped the reins, covered his eyes, and waited to die.

* * * * * *

Enu's eyes opened wide, and his jaw dropped, when he saw the chariots closing in. Too far away for the drivers to hear a shouted warning, too close for the horses to stop in time. All he could think of was to clear as many sheep as possible out of the way. He slapped the wooly backs with his prodding stick to make them move faster, but he might as well have tried to move cold molasses.

He waved to his men to keep back. No use risking human lives as well.

Perceiving the futility of moving the sheep any faster, he saw that the chariots were nearly upon him, so he dove for cover into the dirt by the side of the road and tremblingly awaited the impact.

* * * * * *

"There's going to be a wreck!" cried Angelina.

Abigail covered her eyes. "I can't bear to watch this!" she exclaimed.

Little Ana's eyes grew as round as saucers as she watched the scene at the crossroads in breathless anticipation.

The puppy continued to whimper.

* * * * * *

Thinking quickly, Nicolas realized he didn't want to injure any sheep. He also wanted to avoid injuring the farmers who were herding the animals. If he turned to his right, he would collide with Petrus' chariot, and he didn't want to do that, either.

He was past caring about his own safety. Whatever he did, he could not save himself. His doom appeared unavoidable. He knew that he would be lucky if he lived. Sooner than risk the lives of others, he would sacrifice himself and his horses. This left him only one option.

He guided the horses to turn abruptly to the left, swerving out of the way of the sheep and the shepherds, and heading straight for the stone wall. The horses whinnied loudly in protest at this sudden change of direction, and instinctively dug their hooves into the ground and skidded to a sudden halt, stopping just an inch or two ahead of the large stone structure. The chariot slammed into the rear ends of the horses, causing the beasts to scream in agony, and tilted upward, overturning with a forward motion. The force of the overturning chariot hurled Nicolas against the stone wall, which he struck with the left side of his body, and he dropped into the dirt and knew no more.

* * * * * *

The wreckage was extensive.

The collapsed chariot had landed upside down on top of the horses, nearly crushing portions of their bodies and hurling them to the ground with mighty snaps of breaking equine bone. While the horses screeched in utter pain, the uppermost wheel of the chariot continued to spin, until it came at last to a stop.

Petrus' chariot had plunged straight into the army of sheep. The force of the impact had panicked the now-driverless horses, which had turned on the sheep and struck many of them with their hooves, wounding and killing several of the bleating animals in the process. The chariot managed to topple over to one side, causing one horse to fall on top of the other, crushing the other badly and rendering the horse unable to rise. Meanwhile Petrus had been flung violently from the chariot and had flown into a nearby thornbush.

Bleats of sheep mingled with cries of horses in agonizing pain and shouts of humans for assistance. Confusion reigned at the crossroads.

* * * * * *

"The white team just crashed into the wall!" exclaimed Angelina.

"The black team has collided with the sheep!" cried Abigail.

Ana ran, with the puppy in her arms, back up the hill and over the little fence to where Aunt Marla, too, had been watching. "There's been a terrible accident," the little girl informed her aunt.

"Yes, I know, dear," said Aunt Marla. She called to the two older girls, "Angelina! Abigail! Go into town and fetch Doctor Romano! Meet us at the crossroads as soon as you can."

She filled a knapsack with some strips of cloth for bandages, some healing herbs and ointments, and a skin of water. Then she strapped the bundle to her shoulder. While the two older girls made ready for a hasty trip into Patara, Marla, carrying the knapsack and Ana, who carried the puppy, hurried along the pathway toward the crossroads.

* * * * * *

By the time Dr. Romano arrived on the scene, along with the two girls, a semblance of order had been established, due largely to Marla's ministrations. She had enlisted the help of the still-trembling Enu and his workers to retrieve the bodies of the two unconscious boys and lay them side by side in a clear patch of dirt away from the road. She had then proceeded to bathe and dress any cuts and wounds that she could discern.

A troop of Roman soldiers had come to offer their assistance, righting what was left of the two chariots and putting the suffering animals out of their misery.

"I have never seen anything like it," Enu frenziedly reported to one of the soldiers. "They came flying along the road with no warning, and before I knew it, nearly a dozen of my best sheep had been maimed or slaughtered. Where are the parents of these boys? They ought to be punished for allowing their children to run rampant like this! The two boys should be whipped! Why, I almost died! I almost died!" He nearly went into convulsions, and had to be restrained by the soldier.

"The two boys are nearly dead," put in Marla. "I think they've had their punishment."

Ana, with the puppy still in her arms, stared at the two boys, particularly the golden-haired one. Even though he was still and pale as death, his features held an otherworldly, ethereal quality that the little girl could not help but admire. He looked like the child of a god. She knew instinctively that, whatever misdeeds he may have done, he was a good person, with a kind, benevolent heart, and whether he should live or die, she would remember his face always. As she reflected on these thoughts, the puppy licked her nose.

Abigail, on the other hand, became enraptured with the black-haired boy. To her, he represented everything that could be fine and noble in a human being. The regal set to his jaw, the firmness of his expression (even in repose), and the elegant clothing he wore convinced the girl that this young man had to be the princeliest prince that ever walked the earth. She knew that she would take a liking to him if ever he should awake, and he might possibly grow to like her as well.

As for Angelina, she considered both boys extremely foolish to have attempted such a stunt, and so did not look closely at either one. She simply assisted her aunt in cleaning their wounds and applying the bandages. As for taking any personal interest in a young man, she knew that as the eldest daughter her future on that score had been decided long ago, and though she had never met her betrothed, she had long ago resolved to support the choice made for her by her parents.

Dr. Romano expressed appreciation for the efforts of Marla and her nieces, declaring their nursing efforts to be first-rate. But, he added, more urgent care was needed. "Where are the boys' parents? They need to be informed."

The servants who had been posted by Petrus near the finish line had come running when they heard the commotion. Now one of them came forward and spoke.

"The dark-haired boy is the son of Senator Maximus and his wife," he said. "The other is the son of the rich nobleman Ephanus. I have already sent messengers informing their parents."

"Well done," said the doctor. "These boys must be taken to their beds at once. They are both at death's door. They must be bled."

* * * * * *

When Nicolas regained consciousness, it took him a few moments to figure out where he was. At length he recognized his own room in his parents' house. He lay in his own bed with coarse linen sheets instead of silk. Never in his life had he been so relieved to see his bedchamber.

Next to him on a stool sat Ephanus. His father had leaned over him when the young eyelids had first fluttered open, and now the old grey eyes peered kindly into the young grey ones.

"Father?" murmured Nicolas.

"Yes, it is I," said Ephanus, tenderly.

"Is Mother here?"

"She has scarcely left your bedside for two days, but just now she is at the convent hospital, helping the holy sisters to attend to the sick. There is a terrible plague in the town, and the sisters desperately need everyone who can help, as the infirmary is very full."

Nicolas tried to stretch his legs, but could feel nothing in his left. His left arm he also found he could not move. His injured limbs had been wrapped in splints and bandages. He could feel smaller bandages all over his aching body.

"What—what has happened to me?" he asked.

"There was an accident. You ran your chariot into a stone wall."

"I remember. We had a wager on the race. A thousand gold pieces."

Ephanus shook his head sadly. "My son, will you never learn?" he asked, in a tone that suggested hopelessness.

"Since I crashed, that means Petrus must have won," said Nicolas. "I must pay him the thousand gold pieces."

"Neither of you won," said Ephanus. "You broke an arm and a leg. Petrus is injured, too. He ran his chariot into a flock of sheep."

"Is he injured badly?"

"Both of his legs are broken. You and he will have to spend many months in bed before you can move around normally again. Even then, your joints will always be a little stiff. So says Dr. Romano, and he is one of the best."

"So am I going to get better? I feel awfully weak."

"That is because the doctor bled you until the color drained from your skin. You look as pale as a ghost, Nico. You nearly died, but the doctor said he has bled out all of the bad blood. The blood that remains inside you is healthy blood. You will recover, but it will take a long time."

"And the horses? The chariot?"

"The horses both had to be put to death, they were in such terrible pain. And the chariot may be of value to a dealer in scraps of wood and metal, but it will be of no more use to you as a vehicle to ride in."

The boy heard the underlying censure in Ephanus' words. He knew he alone was to blame, perhaps not for the accident, but for the circumstances that had made such an accident possible. Now he realized that the chariot and horses he was so nobly going to give back to his father were gone for naught. He had not only spent the money foolishly in the first place, he had now wasted it by destroying the things that had been bought with it and left no chance for any of it to be recovered. Nicolas gazed up at his father, full of things to say but unsure how to begin.

"Father," he began, but Ephanus, speaking at the same moment, cut him off.

"Nico, how can you be such a foolish boy? Will you continue to spend my money on worthless trifles, just so that you can appear to be as good as a boy who is arrogant and spoiled?"

"No, Father," said Nicolas, softly but firmly. "That part is over." And he told his father everything—of his nighttime encounter with the living Christ, of his determination to live a better life, and of his understanding of what paying a price really meant. He did not tell about the beating or being locked in a closet by a drunken Sergius, but Nicolas knew his father's shrewdness, and correctly guessed that the older one could fill in the blanks for himself.

Ephanus nodded sagely. He appeared to understand everything, even the things Nicolas could not bring himself to mention.

"Father, I—I'm sorry. I've been a foolish boy, as you have said, but I don't want to be like Petrus anymore, Father. Not ever. He can have his chariots and his horses and his fine clothes and live in a magnificent house. I want a different sort of life. I want to serve the Lord. I want to dedicate my life to helping others, and to giving to others. There are so many who have so little, and we have so much."

"We have more than you will ever know, my son," said Ephanus, trying not to betray too much of the emotion he felt at his child's words. "Now that you have learned your lesson about wealth, I shall die in peace when my time comes."

"Oh, please, Father, don't talk of dying when I have just begun knowing how to live!"

Ephanus smiled. "We live a short life upon this earth, Nico. All of us must die some day, but I am in good health, and though no longer young, I keep myself in good condition. I expect, God willing, that I shall be around for a good many more years to come."

CHAPTER NINE:

Nico Grows Up

The nine-year-old boy placed a bundle of flowers on his father's tombstone and then he placed another on the stone underneath which his mother lay. He could not keep himself from giving way to grief, and he sobbed bitterly, the wintry wind making his eyes sting as the tears flowed.

"I learned my lesson only to lose you, Father," sobbed Nicolas. "Please come back so that you can teach me some more. I'll love you better this time, and I'll be a better son than I ever was. Please come back to me, Father. Please come back to me, Mother." Knowing his request was futile, Nicolas fell face down on the ground of the cemetery and wept.

The plague had ravaged more than half of Lycia before it finally diminished and went away. There seemed to be no cure, for those who fell prey to the disease's symptoms seldom improved, but wasted away until claimed by the grim reaper whose name is Death. Shortly after Nicolas had begun to recover from his injuries, Joana had contracted the disease during her ministrations at the convent hospital. She had not been alone in her misery, for only a handful of the sisters and lay workers had survived. Then Ephanus had caught it from Joana. For safety, Nicolas had been sent to the monastery to be with his uncle—but even that had proved no safe haven, for an alarming number of the monks had also taken ill. Priscila, Petrus' mother, had likewise succumbed to the plague, as had Anabel, the mother of Angelina, Abigail, and Ana. No family, it seemed, went untouched. And now it remained for those left behind to bury and mourn the dead.

A gentle hand rested on Nicolas' shoulder. "Come, Nico," said a deep, solemn voice. "It is time for us to leave. The cold winds of winter are upon us, and we must go back inside."

Nicolas shook his head and continued to lie there, sobbing. "Your parents are not there, child," the voice went on, soothingly. "They are in Heaven, and they are happy. They want you to be happy once again, too."

"I'll never be happy again," muttered Nicolas.

"Never is a long time," said Stephanus, taking the slight, pale hand of the nine-year-old into his thick, pudgy one. "Now up we go, and before we retire for the night, we will stop by the kitchen and see what Brother John has for us to eat." He helped the sobbing boy to his feet and lifted him onto his massive shoulders, carrying him piggyback all the way to the rear entrance of the monastery.

Brother John, as it turned out, had just roasted a fine goose and had concocted his excellent sauce to go with it. This just happened to be young Nicolas' favorite dish, and though at first the boy insisted he wasn't hungry, the aroma from Abbot Stephanus' plateful soon caused him to take an interest in sampling some of the dinner for himself. "Eat up, eat up, my boy," urged Nicolas' uncle. "God loves a hearty eater. A healthy appetite means a healthy body and a healthy mind." He reached over and pinched the boy's cheek affectionately, a gesture that never failed to get a smile from Nicolas. On this night, however, there was no smile.

"You will smile again, Nico," said Uncle Stephanus. "That I promise you. And if you be any kin of mine, I rather think you will bring many smiles to many faces in the years to come."

The boy, having taken a few bites, pushed his plate away. "I miss my father," he said.

"I miss him too," said Stephanus. "He was a rare, good

man, that brother of mine. He did not laugh much, that one, nor did he play many games. I suspect he took life a shade more seriously than Our Lord perhaps intended, but he loved the Lord with all his heart and he gave generously to his fellow man. You couldn't ask for a nobler soul than that. And your mother—why, your mother was a saint, if ever I knew one. Look at how she died—giving her life to help others." A giant tear trickled down his giant cheek, and a fat finger wiped it away.

Brother John poured two mugs of hot cider freshly-brewed from the hearth, to keep the chill away, and after placing one before the Abbot and another before the nephew, he retired to his cell for the night.

Stephanus picked up his mug, raised it to his lips, and swallowed a hot mouthful as though it were nothing at all. He nudged the mug that sat in front of Nicolas, as though urging him to likewise take a drink.

"What would my father tell me now, if he were here?" asked Nicolas, thoughtfully.

Stephanus grinned. "Why, if he were here, your father would tell you to mind his brother while under his care, to eat hearty, to drink hearty, and to start practicing those smiles."

A very faint smile showed on Nicolas' lips. "Those are your words, not his," he said, amused by his uncle's humor despite his grief. "He would tell me to obey God, be a good servant to Christ, and to be a good son—I mean, a good nephew."

"By Heaven, I believe that is exactly what my dear brother would say!" roared Stephanus. "You knew and understood him well."

"I loved him," said Nicolas. He reached for the mug, and took a tentative sip of its contents.

As Nicolas grew, so did his devotion to God. He settled into life at the monastery and soon a daily routine had established itself—one that Stephanus made sure had a hefty amount of time set aside for the boy's schooling. Jocular though he may have been, the Abbot expected his charges to read and write fluent Latin and Greek, and to know the scriptures backward and forward. In addition, he wanted Nicolas to develop a working understanding of medicines and the healing arts, of plant and animal life, of the history of the world, of food and cooking, of fine wines and their making, of geography, of music, and of alchemy and physics. "Knowledge is power," he often said. "The more you know, the more useful you become." Before long, the boy's existence had fallen into a familiar, if not comfortable, pattern. He took his meals with the holy brothers. He had his lessons from Brother Augustus and reported to Brother John in the kitchen for his daily chores.

At Sunday services, Nicolas helped the holy brothers in the serving of the communion wine and the lighting of the candles. Every week, without fail, the nobleman Florus Dorius, who had been a friend of Nicolas' late father, would bring his three girls to mass. Nicolas felt sorry for the children, for they too had lost their mother to the plague. Florus always spoke a kind word to the boy, and inquired as to how he was getting along at the monastery. Nicolas noted that the youngest daughter, whom he considered the prettiest, always gave him a shy smile. Whenever he smiled in return, she would blush and hide behind the skirts of her older sisters.

As for Petrus, whose legs had long since healed, Nicolas saw very little of him, although the two remained firm friends. Now, when they met, the difference in their lifestyles became immediately evident, as Petrus always wore the best and latest fashions, and Nicolas now exclusively wore the only garment available to a resident of the monastery—a black robe, gathered by a rope at the waist, with a black hood. Petrus would tease his erstwhile companion about being an unworldly monk, and Nicolas would counter-tease his friend about being a spoiled, rich brat. Both took it and gave it in good fun and with the greatest possible regard for one another, despite their separate paths.

Nicolas had made a point of paying back every penny of the debt he owed to Sergius, but the latter barely acknowledged the repayment, having endured the much greater loss of his wife. The Magistrate seemed to have lost his senses in the wake of the tragedy, for he scarcely seemed rational on the few occasions when Nicolas saw him. The boy feared, though his friend did not betray it, that the beatings had resumed at a worse rate of frequency than before. But of this the two friends never spoke.

Once a week, as ever, the black-haired boy would arrive with a paltry offering for the poor, which the good monks were obliged to accept gratefully. The sizes of the bundles had diminished considerably since the passing of Petrus' mother, and especially since the father took no part in any Christian rites. The boy's attendance at worship became sporadic. Weeks would pass, but then, startlingly, the princely youth would make his appearance in his Sunday best—driven, as before, in a brand-new magnificent chariot pulled by young Arabian steeds, and wearing, as always, the finest garments money could buy. On these occasions, Nicolas noticed that the middle daughter of Florus' family could not keep her admiring eyes from the dazzling splendor of Petrus' outward show. He couldn't help but sympathize and feel a little sorry for the girl, for like his younger self, she had fallen under the spell of the charmer, not knowing the sordid truth that lay behind the glitter.

As the years passed, Abbot Stephanus' fatherly feelings for the boy deepened, and he yearned for the day when Nicolas would choose a vocation. He naturally had hopes that the boy would elect to serve Christ as a member of the holy brotherhood, but he did not wish to force his nephew into a decision that could turn out to be ill-advised if not undertaken with a sincere heart. It delighted him to see the boy's evident desire to give the things of God priority over the things of the world, but at the same time Nicolas could become so earnest that he seemed always to be weighed down with a burden of cares and concerns. The boy seldom if ever laughed, and though the Abbot did his best to encourage some levity now and then, Nicolas seemed too reverent and solemn to experience or appreciate any lighter moments.

Whenever the boy did chance to smile, or better yet to laugh, Stephanus would offer up a silent prayer of thanks, for Nicolas had a bright, engaging, youthful face and the Abbot strongly felt that the young man should know what joy was like—or the rest of his learning would be for nothing.

To ensure that the young man would have no regrets about giving up a worldly existence, Stephanus made sure that Nicolas had plenty of opportunities to meet girls his own age—especially the lovely daughters of Florus, who grew more comely and womanly with each passing year. He didn't want his nephew to later feel that he had missed out by choosing a life of celibacy. If fleshly desires prevailed and marriage and a family were to be his lot, then the monastery could no longer be a home to him, and yet the uncle could envision a rich, full life for the boy if he should choose the life of a monk.

Daily the Abbot included in his devotions a prayer that his nephew would make the best decision for his life and would follow the path that God had laid out for him, whatever that path might be. By degrees, as the boy grew into a young man and ripened into early maturity, the Abbot saw more and more in his nephew a semblance of the young man he himself had been, as time and again Nico chose the things of God over the things of the world.

Once, he caught Nicolas kneeling in prayer in the chapel. A look of radiance shone over the young man's entire face, making his golden hair appear a veritable halo. Not for the world would the uncle have disturbed the boy's devotions, but the sight confirmed for him that Nicolas had a true calling to live a life in the service of the Lord. The older man crept stealthily away, which was no small feat considering his vast size, and later offered up his own prayer of thanks.

Nicolas seemed never to doubt his vocation from the moment he had come to an acceptance of his parents' death. He carried out each day's tasks with a serving heart, and he willingly attended all required masses and prayer gatherings, even those that were not absolutely mandatory. He felt as though he fit into the life of a monk the way a hand fits into a glove. Having learned so much about the world at an early age, he had little or no appetite for life outside the walls of the monastery. In his forays to the marketplace or to visit the poor or the sick he felt like an outsider to the busy life of the town. However, inside the monastery he felt truly fulfilled, happy, and at peace with God.

His uncle's first confirmation that a decision had already been made in regard to his vocation came on a spring evening when Nicolas was fifteen. The boy entered the Abbot's study with a troubled expression on his face. The Abbot sat in the same spot where he had shown his seven-year-old nephew the Fortunatus purse.

"What is the matter, Nico?" asked Stephanus. "You look as though your heart has fallen down a deep, deep well." He gestured to a chair.

"It has," answered Nicolas. His voice squeaked occasionally, as it had only recently begun to change and deepen. "I feel as though the bottom has dropped out of my world." He sat down in the chair, his long, lanky arms (almost disproportionate to the rest of his body), dangling awkwardly at his sides. He had grown into a stretched-out version of his former self, the cherubic plumpness of his face having given way to a lean, angular jaw line and thinner, paler cheeks.

"Why?" asked Stephanus. "What has happened?"

"I learned from Brother John that I can never be a proper monk," said the young man, sadly, "because I am wealthy, and have inherited my father's entire fortune, and a monk must be poor."

"It is true that we take a vow of poverty," asserted Stephanus, "but you are not ready for your final vows. Why, you are barely a novice. Your fortune will not hinder you from serving as a novice."

"But it will keep me from becoming a true monk, will it not?"

"There is time enough for us to decide what to do about your fortune," said Stephanus, in rough yet soothing tones. "You can dispose of it in any way you see fit."

"I'll—I'll give it away!" declared Nicolas. "I'll distribute every penny to the poor."

Stephanus put up a thick finger. "Now let us be wise about this, Nico. The money your father left you is a living, growing entity. The more it grows, the more money it makes. Every passing year adds more gold to your coffers. To rid yourself of everything could take years of legal proceedings, which still might not be resolved by the time you are an old man. It will not be as easy to rid yourself of it as you might think. Now, if you had a family to give it to—"

"Nobody," groaned Nicolas. "I have no one! You are my only living relative!"

"Now see here," said the Abbot, sternly. "Do not even consider giving it to me. I would have to resign my position immediately, and I have no intention of doing that. No, you must keep it for the present time."

"What will I do when it comes time to take my final vows?"

The Abbot thought for a moment. When thinking deeply, he sometimes rubbed his nose with his large forefinger. His eyes narrowed as he considered the matter thoroughly. A moment later, he nodded and snapped his fingers in confirmation of a solution. "We shall find ways to get rid of the money," promised the Abbot. "But we will do it in stealth and secrecy. Who besides Brother John knows you have inherited your father's fortune?"

"Nobody, except for you and me."

"Splendid!" laughed Stephanus in his usual hearty manner. "Brother John is a known and confessed stretcher of the truth, so his word will not hold water with any of the other monks. You and I will simply say nothing of the matter. You will devise ways to rid yourself of the money secretly. Go into the town and find people who have specific needs. Locate those who have a desperate need for a certain bill to be paid by a certain date. Then discreetly supply the needed amount, and none will ever be the wiser that the good Nico has been their special angel."

"Would—would that be all right? Is—is it honest? In God's eyes, I mean?"

"If it is not boy, may the weight of guilt fall entirely upon me, and not you! I am your Abbot and your spiritual leader. If I say a thing is all right, then it must indeed be godly! Now, let us have no more nonsense about your not becoming a monk! If it is your aptitude, boy, and your calling, then God will make certain you will be accepted. Have no fear!"

At these cheering words, Nicolas could not refrain from a tentative smile, which lit up his uncle's heart on the inside more than the young man ever knew.

CHAPTER TEN:

Petrus' Vocation

With his hood thrown back as usual, and his black robes hanging limply on his lanky body, the sleeves constantly falling forward over his hands, Nicolas presented an incongruous sight as he chopped wood for the kitchen fire. Every time he hefted the great axe, his garment shifted. When he raised it up over his head preparatory to striking the blow, his sleeves fell, leaving his arms exposed and the weight of the robes' excess cloth causing the folds to dangle onto the ground behind his bare feet. When he lowered the axe to strike, the robes fell forward, touching the ground in front of his feet, the sleeves covering his arms and getting tangled with the blade as he attempted to lift the instrument up again. Still he persisted in the chore. His actual chopping, minus the problems with the robes, had improved over the six years he had lived at the monastery, and in good time he chopped the necessary amount of wood.

He had been Brother John's kitchen assistant for as long as he had lived there, and he often wondered why he had been assigned this particular duty. Nothing about it had come easy to him, but he had learned every task with the most willing of hearts, and so had managed to achieve a degree of proficiency at each chore, though never would he consider himself an expert at any of the work. Still, if Abbot Stephanus had placed him there, it must have been for a reason.

There was little love lost between Nicolas and Brother

John. The head of the kitchen often grumbled about his assistant's slowness, inefficiency, and general unfitness for the work, but anytime he did so in the presence of the Abbot, the reverend father would cast a withering glance in the holy brother's direction, and John would fall silent on the matter.

Now, as Nicolas gathered the wood in his arms, he was astonished to find Brother John at his elbow, offering to take in the wood himself. He must have been under special instructions from the Abbot, thought Nicolas, as the brother would never have come forth to do such a task on his own. "You're wanted in the Abbot's private study," growled Brother John in his usual antagonistic tones.

Nicolas thanked the holy brother and rushed to see what his uncle wanted. To his utter amazement, he saw Petrus standing beside Abbot Stephanus. The black-haired young man had grown to a manly stature. However, the years had added a perpetual smirk to his cynical young face. He wore a brightly-colored cloak over a brightly-colored toga and tunic. On his feet was a pair of brand-new sandals. The Abbot wore a pleased and gratified expression.

"Petrus!" exclaimed Nicolas. "What brings you here?"

"I've come to join up," declared Petrus, in a decided tone of voice. His voice had deepened much earlier than Nicolas,' as it had a manly resonance now, and it didn't squeak, as Nicolas' still occasionally did.

Nicolas felt mystified. "Join up? What do you mean? I—I don't understand."

"He wants to become a member of our order," explained the Abbot.

"You? Oh, Petrus, I don't think—"

"Brother Nico," said Petrus, "you do not have a monopoly on the spiritual life. Surely, there is room in the kingdom of God for one more faithful servant?"

"Why, yes, yes, of course," stammered Nicolas. "But are you ready? I don't recall that you were ever very religious.

I mean, I know that your mother was a Christian, and so are you—?"

"Is my Christianity in doubt? Is that what you mean?" asked Petrus, giving his old friend a special display of his well-developed smirk.

"No," said Nicolas. "But, Petrus, you'll have to give up all of your worldly possessions. Your beautiful horses . . . your magnificent chariot . . . your fine clothes . . . they will all have to go. Can you do that?"

"You did it," said Petrus, "and the Lord only knows you gave up much more wealth than I will ever know. If you can live a life of poverty, chastity, and selfless dedication to a higher calling, then why on earth can't I?"

"I never said you couldn't," said Nicolas. "It's only . . . I'm surprised, that's all. Petrus, why?"

For a moment only, Petrus dropped his showoff attitude and revealed a trace of sincerity. "You're so happy and fulfilled, Nico. You have found your calling in serving Christ. Well, I want to be happy and fulfilled, too. I likewise want to serve Christ."

Still feeling overwhelmed and perplexed by the suddenness of his friend's decision, Nicolas cast a bewildered eye at his uncle. "Are you—do you—do you support—?"

"Of course, I am happy to welcome any devoted son of the church to help him find his true vocation." He winked at his nephew. "I think it is excellent that you two friends shall be holy brothers together."

Petrus grinned. "Now we are well and truly brothers," he said, repeating the phrase he had used so often in their childhood.

Nicolas sighed. "Very well," he said.

"And *you* will be in charge of his training," said the Abbot, pointing a thick finger at Nicolas.

"Me?" protested Nicolas. "But—I am not qualified to train him."

"As Head Novice, you have full authority over him—answerable only to Brother John and to myself."

"Since when am I the Head Novice, Father Abbot?" asked Nicolas, in surprise.

"Since right now. I have just promoted you. Now run along, Brother Nicolas, and teach Brother Petrus his duties. There is much work to be done. I have my work, and you young men have yours." With that, the Abbot shoved them out of his study and shut the door.

Still perplexed, Nicolas led the way down the corridor to the monks' quarters. The events of the past few minutes had mystified him entirely, yet he had been given no choice but to make the best of it. So he explained as Petrus followed him.

"My uncle was only jesting when he gave us the title of 'Brother.' We won't become holy brothers until we have taken our final vows and been accepted into the ministry for life." He stopped and turned to look at his friend. "Are—are you *really* sure you want to do this?" he asked.

"Positive," declared Petrus.

"I said for life. It's a lifetime commitment. You do realize that."

"I know, I know."

Resignedly, still certain his friend was making a mistake, Nicolas brought Petrus past the cells where the monks slept, and led his friend to an unoccupied room next to his own in the novices' quarters. The room contained only a bed, a chair, and a candle. Over the doorway hung a cross.

"This is where you will sleep," said Nicolas, expecting a comment on the tiny chamber's drab simplicity.

"All right," said Petrus, agreeably. "What do I do first?"

"You must remove those clothes—the cloak, everything," directed Nicolas. "While you are undressing, I will fetch a robe for you."

Moments later, when Nicolas returned, half expecting to find that his friend had fled rather than sacrifice his finery, he found Petrus waiting for him, his fine clothes in a neat pile. The black-haired young man needed no assistance in pulling on the black robe and securing it around his waist by means of a piece of rope. By luck, Nicolas had managed to get a garment that was neither too big—as was his own—nor too small. The robe fit Petrus as though it had been tailored especially for him.

Nicolas gathered up his friend's former clothing into a bundle, and started to carry it away. "Where are you going?" asked Petrus, showing, at last, some concern over his personal belongings.

"I'm taking these clothes to Brother Zephanius, the one who procured your robe for me," explained Nicolas. "He will arrange to have them given to those in need."

"My clothes are being donated to the poor?" asked Petrus, appearing surprised for the first time that day. "My fine cloak, and my elegant toga, and my hardly-worn sandals?"

Nicolas nodded.

"Oh," said Petrus, thoughtfully.

"You are *sure* you want to go through with this?" queried Nicolas, firmly.

"Of course, of course," said Petrus.

The new Head Novice started off. "Wait here," he instructed as he left.

"Nico . . ."

Nicolas paused at the top of the stairs. "What is it?"

"What will I wear when I—that is, if I—" He seemed unable to finish.

"When you leave the monastery? Is that what you're try-ing to say?" asked Nicolas. "You're *not* leaving, remember? You're going to live here now for the rest of your life. You *do* understand that, don't you?"

"Well, I . . . yes, yes! Of course. I didn't know what I was saying. No, I do understand. I won't need my clothes anymore. It's just that . . . I've never devoted my life to God before, you know. It's all new to me."

"It isn't too late to change your mind," said Nicolas. "But once these clothes are gone—you won't get them back again."

"Stop saying things like that!" snapped Petrus, irritably. "Of course I know what I'm doing! I'm not going to change my mind! Besides, if you can live this way, so can I."

"Is that what this is all about?" Nicolas felt himself getting more than a little irritated. "Are you trying to emulate me, the way I tried once to emulate you? We don't always have to have the same things, you know. We can be friends and still live different lives. I don't think you will be happy here, my friend. I think you should go back home to your father."

"NO!" exclaimed Petrus, vehemently. "I can't . . . I mean, I couldn't . . . I mean . . . oh, Nico, this is the kind of life I want more than anything! I want to renounce all worldly goods and live a holy and simple life. I can do this. I know I can."

"Suit yourself," said Nicolas. "Then wait for me while I get rid of this bundle. After that, we will go to the kitchen and I will teach you what to do."

"Teach me. Please teach me," begged Petrus.

Nicolas shrugged and went down the stairs.

If Brother John had seemed put out before, now he had double the reason for being cross most of the time. He now had two kitchen apprentices, one twice as inept as the other. Petrus proved more of a hindrance than a help in any chore. He didn't know how to do anything, and he turned out to be a poor learner. He could not chop wood. He could not lay a fire. He could not even put a kettle of water over the fire without spilling the entire contents and dousing the flames. The more Nicolas tried to teach him, the worse he got.

The only thing he demonstrated an aptitude for was prayer. He learned his prayers much faster than Nicolas ever could, and he memorized the scriptures with a rapidity that the golden-haired novice envied. He often appeared not to be paying attention at masses, and yet could later recite the entire service almost word for word. The same held true for Abbot Stephanus' sermons and homilies. Petrus could repeat back every one of them with incredible exactitude.

This ability impressed the Abbot, who insisted that the young man remain on kitchen duty, confident that the holy brother and the Head Novice eventually would find something practical that Petrus was capable of doing.

Soon it became evident that Petrus did indeed have a penchant for something, and that was mischief. His practical jokes made him the bane of everyone else's existence. It all started with the shoes.

Abbot Stephanus, himself possessed of somewhat tender feet, did not forbid the wearing of shoes or sandals. Though generally in short supply, a few pairs of shoes were available for those who had need of them. Most of the brothers chose to go barefoot voluntarily, at least during the temperate months, as a token of humility and devotion, as likewise did the novice Nicolas. Petrus, on the other hand, after a few shoeless days, fell into the habit of never going anywhere without something on his feet. The trouble was, the shoes he wore did not appear appropriate for one who was expected to take permanent vows of poverty. In truth, he had sent word to a servant in his father's house to fetch a pair of his best shoes, and these he now wore openly.

Brother John greatly resented the shoes. Watching the black-haired young man ineptly attempting to perform his chores was bad enough, but seeing the finest shoes money could buy on a pair of—to Brother John—utterly useless feet, proved more than the brother of the kitchen could bear. When Petrus, for the thousandth time, had spilled a cauldron of soup, thus effectively dousing the kitchen fire, Brother John roared at him to take off the shoes and perform his chores in something more suitable. When the young man gave a look of defiance, Brother John slapped his face and told him he was completely unfit to be a monk. Hot tears of anger filled Petrus' eyes, and he fled from the kitchen.

Nicolas, who had silently witnessed the scene, ran to Petrus' room to comfort him. He found the shoes flung into a corner, and his companion sobbing bitterly.

"It was wrong of Brother John to yell at you," said Nicolas, soothingly. "He had no business saying you were unfit. Such a matter is for you alone to decide. You and Father Stephanus. And God, of course."

"They hate me! They all hate me here!" sobbed Petrus. "No matter what I do, I can't win."

"That's just part of life here," said Nicolas. "They'll get used to you in time. I think."

"What's wrong with wearing shoes? My feet blister easily."

"It wasn't the shoes," pointed out Nicolas, "it was the *kind* of shoes. Where did you manage to find them, anyway? It is very seldom anyone gives us such elegant footwear."

"They're mine," explained Petrus. "Mine from home. I found I couldn't bear being without a pair of good, sturdy shoes that fit me."

"Petrus," said Nicolas, "you have to put your former life behind you now. Don't you understand? You're serving God."

"Wouldn't God want me to have a good pair of shoes?"

Nicolas couldn't help smiling. "Of course He would. I don't blame you for wanting to have something from home with you. And it's probably all right for now, at least until you take your vows. So keep them, until someone tells you otherwise. In the meantime, why don't you put the shoes away and save them for special occasions, and find yourself a more ordinary-looking pair? I'll even help you look for some decent ones."

Petrus gave his friend a grateful nod. Then, as he straightened up, sniffed, and wiped away his tears, he grew self-conscious. "I'm so ashamed of myself. Look at me, fifteen years old and blubbering like a baby!"

"It all takes getting used to, Petrus," said Nicolas. "This whole way of living is different for you. I've seen it building up for a long time. You had to let it out, but cheer up now, won't you? Let's get the shoes and then get back to our chores."

Noticing how easily Nicolas rose from the floor and moved down the corridor with nothing on his feet, Petrus remarked on it. "How do you and the others manage it?" he asked. "Aren't your feet all bruised and bloody by the end of the day?"

"Not at all," said Nicolas, picking up his left foot with his left hand and turning the sole upward so that Petrus could see it. He tapped on the rough, leathery surface with the fingers of his right hand. "You see that? Tough as rock. Of course, I've been here for six years, but your feet will also toughen up, given time."

Petrus appeared thoughtful as he walked down the stairs.

They picked out a pair of shoes that Petrus found he could wear with some degree of comfort and then returned to their work. Brother John scolded them for having been gone so long, and soon everything got back to normal.

Nicolas thought that the incident was over, but the next morning when he and Brother John arrived in the kitchen to prepare breakfast, they found that the smooth stone floor had been liberally covered with sharp rocks and thorns. Brother John howled with pain after taking a step and Nicolas winced as he reached down to pull out a sharp thorn that had embedded itself in his heel. The holy brother knew at once who had done it, and slapped Nicolas for suspected complicity.

The golden-haired novice rubbed his cheek angrily. "If you hadn't been so cruel to him, this wouldn't have happened," he snapped, though knowing full well he would have to do penance for his words. Then he grabbed a broom and started sweeping.

The black-haired novice did not show his face all day. He could not be found in his bed, in the chapel, or in any known nook or corner in the monastery. When he did finally put in an appearance at evening prayer, Brother John waited until the prayer had finished, then grabbed his wayward apprentice by the back of the neck and hauled him into the kitchen to spend the night scrubbing pots and pans.

"Where did you go?" asked Nicolas early the next morning, when a weary-eyed Petrus trudged upstairs to get some sleep in the ten minutes before matins.

The unrepentant Petrus managed a faint grin of triumph. "To do something pleasant, for a change," was the only answer he would give.

The something pleasant became evident by the following Sunday. After a week of cleaning the monastery stables—a chore that invariably went to whoever had committed the most grievous offense the week before—Petrus had feared he would smell of manure for the rest of his life. However, Nicolas noted that his friend had found some way to get himself spruced up and clean-smelling for Sunday mass.

At the conclusion of the service, the two young men with their hoods thrown back in the bright spring sunshine stood on the steps of the church near Father Stephanus, and all three cordially nodded to the departing parishioners. The nobleman Florus greeted the Abbot and, as always, spoke a special word to Nicolas. The three daughters stood at a respectful distance.

When he looked closely at Petrus, Florus spoke to the dark-haired novice. "I have seen you here for several weeks," he observed, "but I did not recognize you until now. You are the son of Sergius Maximus, the Magistrate, are you not?"

Petrus nodded.

"Your father and Nicolas' late father were two of my closest and best friends," said Florus. "I trust your father is well? I was grieved to hear of the loss of his wife, your mother."

"That was six years ago," said Petrus, as though the deep-voiced young man of today and the nine-year-old child who had cried himself to sleep every night back then were two different people.

"My own dear wife passed away that year, also," said

Florus, in a solemn tone of voice. "It was a terrible time for us all. I am glad to see you looking well. Give my regards to your father when you see him."

"I never see him," said Petrus, darkly, momentarily averting his eyes. "He is not a Christian, and I—I am." This last assertion seemed to stick in his throat.

"In any event, you will doubtless flourish in your calling. Nicolas thrives in the monastic life. I can see it in the radiant glow in his face." He smiled at the golden-haired novice, who self-consciously smiled back. "You, young Maximus, already possess quite a holy and noble bearing. The black robes suit you well. He must possess quite an aptitude, Father."

"Oh, yes," said Stephanus. "He has an aptitude . . . we just don't know what it is yet!"

Florus laughed. "He is young. There is plenty of time. By the way, Father, I have news I haven't told you yet. My eldest daughter, Angelina, is to be married at New Year's."

"That is excellent news!" exclaimed Stephanus. "My heartiest congratulations to you and your entire family. Who is the blessed and fortunate young man?"

The nobleman waved to a pair of young men who had been standing awkwardly off to one side for several minutes. The two came forward at Florus' signal. One was tall and slender with dark brown hair and a very regal bearing. His thin mustache and beard made him appear much older than his true age, which Nicolas guessed to be about eighteen. The other was shorter and much younger, with similar chestnut-brown hair, slightly tinged with a reddish hue. Both wore fur-lined cloaks, though the spring weather made the day mild and pleasant.

"This is Prince Korin Koratovich, and his brother, Prince Ilyan," introduced Florus. "They are visitors from the Slavic city of Novgorod in the northern country. Prince Korin is to be my Angelina's husband."

Abbot Stephanus bowed low. "Your Royal Highnesses," he murmured.

Prince Korin spoke. "We are noble princes, not royalty," he corrected.

"At any rate, you are welcome to my humble parish," said the Abbot, sincerely. He in turn introduced the princes to the two novices. Nicolas detected a flash of hostility in the look Petrus fixed on the elder of the Slavs. Prince Korin likewise appeared to take an instant dislike to the raven-haired novice. Only later did Nicolas come to understand why these two should detest each other on first sight.

Prince Korin seemed extraordinarily tall to Nicolas, although the sense of height might have been augmented by the young Slav's slender figure. Korin's dark brown hair, beard, and mustache contrasted with the pallor of his skin, the latter likely a result of the long sunless northern winters. His facial features, with his high cheekbones and long, slender nose, could have been carved out of stone or marble. He had an air of perfection about him. His physical appearance as well as his general manner indicated impeccable correctness, which were reflected in his faultlessly erect posture and in the flawless arrangement of his clothing. A plumed hat adorned his head. Draped over his shoulders, and gathered below the neck with a jeweled brooch, a jet-black cloak flowed with exquisite symmetry down the prince's back to mid-calf length. The garment was magnificent in its simplicity and lined underneath with grey fur that must have come from the hide of a bear or a wolf. His tunic, of the deepest indigo, the black breeches that hugged his slender legs, and a pair of thick fur-lined boots completed his ensemble.

Ilyan, the Prince's younger brother, looked like a smaller, shorter version of Korin, except for the reddish tinge to his hair, a healthy flush to his cheeks, and the fact that the boy had no beard. Though the princeling was as finely dressed as his brother, Ilyan's courtly grace and demeanor appeared more natural and less studied.

The Abbot drew his friend Florus away on pretext of making plans for the wedding, which hardly entailed any pressing business as it lay many months away. Nicolas knew that he had done this to give the young people a chance to converse more freely, and to ensure that his two protégés would get a taste of what they would be giving up in the years to come.

After an icy greeting to Petrus, and an only slightly more civil one to Nicolas, Prince Korin took the eldest daughter, Angelina, to one side and conversed in low tones with her. The arrangement for the wedding, planned by their fathers, appeared an agreeable prospect to both of them, and the two together looked as though they belonged to each other. Both, reflected Nicolas, seemed a bit aloof and distant from everybody else, and the looks they were giving to one another suggested that despite the marriage's having been an arranged one, it couldn't have been a more suitable match.

He turned to observe Petrus puffing up his cheeks and blowing out the air with audible breaths. His friend's face had gotten red as a beet. "What are you doing?" asked Nicolas.

"Never mind," he muttered. "Have you spoken to the girls yet?" he asked, changing the subject quickly.

"No, I—" Nicolas had been about to say that he thought too much friendliness with young ladies was not the right sort of behavior for a monk-in-training when Petrus grabbed his arm and whisked him over to where Abigail and Ana stood shyly whispering.

Abigail's figure had filled out in womanly fashion, although she still lacked her fourteenth birthday. She had a tendency to plumpness, but the roundness of her face and figure only added to her winsome appeal. Her smile always grew brighter in the presence of Petrus, who now stood quite close to her.

Though only eleven, little Ana showed promise of greater beauty than either of her two sisters, or so Nicolas thought. She had dark, curly hair and a small, porcelain-like face with greenish, expressive eyes as mysterious as those of a cat. When she smiled, she looked as though her face were a candle that could light the whole world. Someday, thought Nicolas, *some fortu-*

nate young man is going to fall in love with her. It will be all I can do to keep from falling in love with her myself.

"So your sister is to be married," said Petrus to the middle daughter, in a sneering tone.

"Yes," said Abigail. "She has found a man she considers good enough for her at last."

"A great pity," said Petrus, scornfully. "It is unfortunate she had to send to the northern country to make her choice. She might have had her pick of any number of men right here in Patara."

"The princes' father and our father were good friends," explained Ana. "This arrangement was made between our parents long ago."

"She never mentioned it to me," muttered Petrus.

"Why should she?" asked Nicolas. "You have nothing to do with the matter."

"I don't, do I?" observed Petrus, with a contemptuous sniff. He glanced at Angelina and the Prince, then turned his attention to the fine shoes on his feet, which he still always wore on Sundays and special occasions.

"Come, Ana," urged Abigail. "It is time we left the holy brothers to their monastic duties. They have more important things to do than dally with girls."

Petrus looked the middle sister in the eye. "We're not holy brothers," he declared firmly. "Not yet, anyway."

"But you soon will be," said Abigail, taking her sister by the hand and walking a few steps away. Not too many steps, just a few.

"Be that as it may, we have no present obligations," said Petrus. "No obligations to anyone."

"Except to us!" laughed Ana. "We saved your lives, you know."

This was news to Nicolas and Petrus. "How? When?" they asked.

Ana explained. "When you two were boys, and you got

into that terrible chariot accident, we watched it from the hillside. We saw it happen."

"I helped fetch the doctor," said Abigail.

"And I made the bandages and cleaned your wounds," said Ana. "I feared you would both die. The doctor said you might never walk again. It's so good to see that he was wrong. I have long wanted to ask after your injuries. You did both heal all right?"

"I am still stiff in my left leg," said Nicolas.

"And I have occasional pain in both legs," confessed Petrus.

"Whatever made you run such a race?" asked Abigail.

Both spoke at the same time. "A wager," said Petrus. "Foolishness," said Nicolas.

The girls laughed. "You raced for different reasons, then," said Abigail. "If you couldn't even agree on the purpose, it's no wonder you smashed up. You should have planned your route more carefully. Why, if we hadn't happened to be watching, you might not have gotten help as soon as you did."

"So you see," said Ana, "you are under a bit of an obligation to us."

"I promise," said Nicolas, solemnly, "if ever I can do a good turn for you or your family, I will."

The smile Ana gave him warmed his heart, and while the thought crossed his mind that a good life could be lived outside the monastery walls as well as within, he did not give such a reflection serious consideration. It was only the kind of thought that any young man might have on a lovely spring day with pretty girls close at hand.

Petrus had by now drawn very close to Abigail. To Nicolas' startled eyes, the dark-haired novice's hands rested just under the girl's womanly breasts, fondling and caressing their way upward. Some very un-monk-like things seemed ready to happen. Nicolas was thankful that from where she stood, little Ana's view was blocked by the folds of the pair's garments.

Abigail herself did not move, but appeared poised and ready for any sort of adventure that might befall.

This isn't right, thought Nicolas, and he averted his eyes. He felt he should do something, but didn't know what. He was too flustered to think.

"The New Year will be doubly festive," said Abbot Stephanus, moving close to the group of young people, and bringing Florus with him. Prince Korin and Angelina followed slowly.

Petrus discreetly yet abruptly moved away, although he put little actual distance between himself and the apparent object of his affections. Abigail continued to cast flirtatious eyes in the young man's direction. Nicolas felt himself getting hot. It seemed to him that the entire order had been about to be disgraced.

While the social graces flowed in the conversation of the others, Nicolas leaned over and whispered to his friend. "What was that all about?"

"Nothing," whispered Petrus in return.

"It didn't look like nothing from where I stood," returned Nicolas, accusingly. "Are you crazy?"

"No. I'm human."

"Brothers have been defrocked and sent packing for less."

"Come off it! Nothing happened! Was there even time for anything to happen? Besides, you weren't doing too badly yourself."

Nicolas took a deep breath. "What do you mean?"

"I saw the way you were looking at the child. Will you not admit you have feelings for her?"

"My feelings were inside me. You were the one actually *doing* the feeling."

"You won't tell, will you? Because if you do, I'll say you did whatever you say I did."

"That's blackmail!"

"No, it isn't. It's sweet!" A grin spread across Petrus' face. "Sweet for me, at least!"

" . . . isn't that right, Nicolas?" asked the Abbot, and Nicolas had to agree with whatever had been said before because he hadn't heard it.

Minutes later, the nobleman and his family group departed. Angelina clung to the arm of the tall Prince. Abigail leaned against her father, who walked with his arm around his middle daughter, and she cast a disappointed look in Petrus' direction, while Nicolas noted with a pang of envy that the youngest Prince and Ana walked off together chatting amiably. Servants ushered them all into a magnificent chariot, and they drove away.

Petrus kept his eyes on the spot where they had been long after the chariot had left. His cheeks were flushed and hot. Nicolas' jaw had dropped open, though he remained unconscious of the fact for several moments. Both appeared hot and bothered.

Abbot Stephanus laughed out loud at the sight of the two breathless young men. Nicolas rightly guessed that his uncle's shrewd eyes had gauged an accurate measure of the situation, and the Abbot flashed his nephew a look that told him it was better for such things to happen now than later.

"Come, you two would-be monks!" chided the Abbot. "Have you no chores or prayers on this holy Sabbath day?"

"Yes, Father," said Petrus.

"Yes, Father," said Nicolas.

The novices hurried off.

CHAPTER ELEVEN:

Disgrace

Easter Sunday was to be a day of feasting, following a two-day fast beginning on the morning of Good Friday, in commemoration of the resurrection's coming after the crucifixion and death of Christ. In preparation, Brother John worked his two apprentices harder than either had worked before. They made every possible delicacy for the occasion—bread, stews, sauces, spices, and honey cakes that had become one of Brother John's specialties. For four days a heavenly aroma filled the air. Then the kitchen activity ceased for two days.

During the fast, only the most needful of chores were to be performed. Most activity was suspended to allow time for meditation and prayer. Nicolas always loved this part of the year, for the two days before Easter gave him a chance to think on the Lord's sacrifice, and the day itself caused him to experience the joy of new life and to contemplate afresh the meaning of Christ's resurrection. The abundance of food after fasting made him think of the prospect of Heaven after life on earth.

Good Friday progressed as normal. Even Petrus offered no complaint about eating no food for such a long stretch of time.

At matins on the Saturday, Nicolas, whose stomach had begun to complain since he had awakened that morning, felt nothing but admiration for his friend's fortitude. Petrus kept his eyes either on the cross or closed as he murmured the words of the prayers in unison with the holy brothers. The devotion that Nicolas sometimes suspected of being a sham appeared, on occasions like this, to be genuine indeed.

On their way out of the chapel, as the monks filed back to their cells to devote the day to prayer, Petrus grabbed the sleeve of Nicolas' robe and pulled him out of the flow of the rest of the traffic.

"What's the matter?" asked Nicolas.

Petrus waited until the brothers had gone, then dragged his friend down the corridor that led to the kitchen.

"But we have no kitchen chores today," protested Nicolas. "Brother John is not even there."

"Exactly," said Petrus. "Let's go. I'm hungry."

"We're not to touch food until tomorrow. You know that."

"I don't care. I want to eat something now."

"Petrus! We can't!"

"Who's going to stop us? Everyone else is in prayer."

Petrus pushed open the door to the kitchen and the two novices crept inside. Knowing exactly where every delicacy had been put in readiness for tomorrow's feast, the black-haired young man opened the cupboard where the cakes had been stored. He greedily seized one and began eating it.

"Petrus, no!" cried Nicolas, in a whisper. "Brother John will see to it that we are severely punished!"

"Don't you want a bite? These are awfully good." Petrus waved a honey cake under Nicolas' nose.

"No, of course not . . ." murmured Nicolas. But just then his stomach growled mightily.

"Come on, you're hungry. I know you're hungry."

Nobody else on the face of the earth could have persuaded him, but when Petrus exercised his charms, it proved more than a hungry fifteen-year-old boy could endure. He craved earnestly, desperately, to eat something. And here were all of those cakes in front of him.

"All right," said Nicolas, warily but hungrily. He helped himself to the biggest, tastiest-looking cake he could find. It tasted so good that he had to have another. And another.

"I'm thirsty now," announced Petrus, after having eaten about ten of the cakes. He went down the stairs that led to the wine cellar and returned a moment later with two bottles.

"That's the Communion wine!" exclaimed Nicolas. "We can't touch that!"

"It's very good," declared Petrus, removing the cork and drinking directly from the bottle. He wiped his mouth and handed the bottle to Nicolas, who had begun to feel thirsty himself. Without even stopping this time to consider the consequences, Nicolas drank. And drank. And drank some more. Pretty soon, what they were doing didn't seem so bad. Nicolas even thanked Petrus for having brought him to share in this private feast.

By the time they had finished two bottles and most of the cakes, both of them felt in a hymn-singing mood, so they raised their voices together in a cacophony of sound, their voices blending together like screeching cats on a fence, their words slurring. Since neither one could stand on his feet, they leaned against the wall, seated on the floor, each with an arm around the other's shoulder, and sang loudly as they finished the last of the cakes.

Abbot Stephanus, hearing the commotion, found them in the kitchen, singing together and having a grand time, cake crumbs on their faces and wine stains on their lips, two empty bottles lying on the floor, and the cupboard empty. He stood staring at them in disgust for several minutes before they knew he was there.

"H'lo, Father," greeted Petrus, cheerfully. "Shorry I can't ge' up. Shomething seemsh to be wrong wi' my legsh."

"Shorry, Father," said Nicolas, with a shamefaced grin.

The Abbot was not smiling.

Though Stephanus deferred their punishment until the day after Easter, the two novices felt a palpable chill from the icy stares of the holy brothers during the Resurrection Day services. Nobody would speak one word to either of them, and both felt tainted with terrible feelings of guilt and shame. The atmosphere did not improve during the feast, as far as the two young men were concerned. They had to content themselves with small helpings of leftover scraps, and conversation all around them in which they could take no part. They were in disgrace, and they knew it.

However, the glares of the brothers were as nothing compared to the lecture administered to them by the Abbot on the following Monday morning. He gave the pair of them a tongue-lashing that made the physical one delivered by Sergius Maximus all those years ago seem like nothing at all. When he had finished, he dismissed Petrus to go directly to his quarters and remain there. He bade Nicolas stay.

"Just who is supposed to be training whom?" he asked, sternly.

Eyes on the floor, Nicolas could not bring himself to speak.

"I thought you had more sense, Nico. I am very ashamed of you."

"I am sorry."

"Being sorry doesn't make up for the thousand and one rules you and your companion have broken. When are you two ever going to learn you cannot become each other? You are you and he is he . . . why do you not understand that? You should have been the one in charge of the situation, not he. You deliberately allowed him to compromise your very position here."

Nicolas raised his eyes imploringly. "You can't mean . . . oh, no, Father. I cannot think of—please, give me another chance. Please!"

"If I really thought you didn't belong here, no amount of pleading would have any effect. But I know your heart, and I think I know his as well. Just now I can't see casting you young hooligans out into the unsuspecting town of Patara to wreak greater havoc, so I will permit you to stay, but only if you will submit to severe punishment."

"I will accept it," said Nicolas humbly. "And I won't break the rules again."

"It is *Petrus* who is being punished for breaking the rules. *You* knew better. I am punishing *you* for being deliberately stupid! Do you understand me?"

"Yes, Father," said Nicolas, in a voice so soft as to be almost inaudible.

Brother John requested and was granted permission to flog, but with the humane provisos that only five lashes of the whip should be administered apiece and that no blood should be drawn. So it befell that Nicolas and Petrus found themselves in the courtyard with their torsos bare and their wrists lashed to whipping-posts, surrounded by the holy brothers and the other novices, who had been summoned to witness an example of what happened to those who flouted the rules. Brother John wielded the whip with much relish, or so the two young men imagined.

"Why is it—ouch!—that whenever I listen to you—ouch!—I get into—ouch!—terrible trouble?" Nicolas managed to gasp out between blows.

"Nobody ever said—ouch!—you have to listen—ouch!—to me—ouch!" cried Petrus.

For the next seven or eight weeks, the two young men found themselves performing every last chore that nobody else cared to touch with a ten-foot pole, chiefly including disposing of human and animal waste. Two other novices were assigned to the kitchen, and the smug grins Brother John gave his former assistants in passing indicated that these two new ones were proving more than satisfactory. Besides the scorn of Brother John, the young men had to endure the derision of the others, who called them The Pig Keepers and The Manure Twins as well as far worse epithets that stretched the limits of what should come from the mouths of holy men. Not only were they in deep disgrace, the boys also spent their days mired ankle-deep in excrement.

They had to take their meals apart from the others, for none of the men could abide their perpetual stench, and part of their punishment was that both were forbidden to bathe. So on life went, the days dragging by slowly, and each responded in his heart to the prolonged penance in his own way. For Nicolas, it made his resolve toward godliness ever firmer. For Petrus, it confirmed his worst fears about the monastic life, and served to make him bitter and resentful toward those he blamed for his predicament.

"It isn't fair!" he grumbled, around the fortieth or fiftieth day of their punishment, while they sat at a generous remove from the others in the dining hall and ate from the leftover scraps.

"You were the one who wanted to break the rules," Nicolas reminded him.

"Don't give me that!" snapped Petrus. "You're just as guilty as I am. You went right along with it, and you ate as much as I did and drank as much, too. Maybe more."

"You are right," said Nicolas meekly, his face burning with shame.

At times like this, Nicolas could hardly bear to look his uncle in the eye, though had he dared cast a glance across the dining hall in the Abbot's direction, he would have seen an occasional pitying, kindly-disposed look whenever Stephanus turned to observe his wayward nephew.

The days crawled. It seemed as though they had done penance forever, when in reality it had been nine weeks. At last, they reached the point where one week remained of their punishment. That one week, however, loomed ahead seemingly longer than all of the previous weeks put together. To Nicolas and Petrus, relief might as well have been a year away for all the good it did them at that moment. Knowing that the end lay just ahead made the last days pass more slowly than ever. Both by this time felt almost as numb in their hearts and souls as they felt in their arms and legs. They went about their daily tasks like zombies.

The teasing had gotten out of hand. Nicolas felt certain that Stephanus had no idea how cruel the other novices and the monks could be. Crude, filthy, ugly phrases were hurled at the two young men, things Nicolas could never have brought himself to repeat. Petrus sometimes found the tongue to give back as good as he got, but no amount of retorts on his part could alter the fact that he and his companion lived and worked among the pigs' excrement. Frequently the insults continued until both young men's eyes stung with hot, angry tears. It was on these occasions that Petrus would shout something equally filthy at the others, but the tormentors would only laugh and resume their daily tasks.

A wordless agreement had sprung up between the two friends. Having spent so much time in the exclusive company of one another, each had developed a strong sense of what the other was thinking, and this, coupled with gestures and facial expressions, enabled them to communicate with little or no spoken exchange. Both understood by the ninth week that they had reached the breaking point with regard to the teasing, and that no one, monk or novice, lay person or priest, would insult them one more time without consequence. Neither cared any longer what punishment might follow. Since they had been living in disgrace for weeks, a few more weeks surely wouldn't matter. Even Nicolas' conscience had failed to gain mastery on this issue, with personal honor and personal integrity at stake.

On one afternoon in early summer, this breaking point found its outlet. A group of novices, who before had taken orders from Nicolas, teased and derided the two penitents until neither could stand it any longer. It was at this point that the look of agreement flashed between them, as they continued to shovel piles and piles of muddy filth.

"Hello." The voice was young, and heavy with a foreign

accent. The voice called to them from over the fence. This was not the side of the fence from which the brothers and novices had done their tormenting. This side of the fence faced the town, a point of view from which many passersby had stopped to watch the two disgraced novices wallowing in their penance. Though the insults from this direction were few and far between, as the townspeople in general did not know their names or the reason for the punishment, their scorn and derision came through as clearly as if they had shouted the vilest comments imaginable.

Nicolas and Petrus turned their heads to see who had addressed them. Right away, Nicolas knew the boy. It was the younger of the Slavic princes who were staying with the Dorius family. The young man, about the age of the two novices, had reddish-brown hair and a milky-white, smooth complexion. He wore a fancy feathered hat with a plume in it, and around his shoulders hung a magnificent gold-trimmed cloak of midnight blue. It had been such a long time since Nicolas had seen or worn anything as fancy that his memory at once raced back to the days when his parents had been alive and he had been trying to match the peacock appearance of his best friend. The pang of remorse that he felt for a moment made his next actions, when he considered the situation much later, seem reprehensible, no matter how justified he may have felt at the time.

"It's the young Prince!" snarled Petrus, scornfully. "Have you come to tease and torment us, too?"

"Please, call me Ilyan," said the young man. "You have not been seen in the services for many weeks, and certain young ladies have been worried about you. They sent me today expressly to make inquiries. What are you doing?"

Petrus picked up a soggy piece of waste. "What do you think we're doing?" he asked. "We're making pies. Mud pies!" He patted and packed the material in his hand until it had formed a somewhat mushy ball. He winked at Nicolas, who unhesitatingly did the same.

"But what for?" asked the mystified young Slav.

"This!" shouted Petrus, and on the word, both he and Nicolas flung their filth-balls as hard as they could, pelting Ilyan in the face and knocking off his hat.

The startled young man turned to flee. "Oh, no you don't," cried Nicolas. The two novices ran to the fence, each grabbing an arm, and hauled the finely-dressed young prince over the wall, hurling him face down into the filthy, muddy pile. Once they had shoved his face into it, they proceeded to rub more of it all over his back, giving him a veritable bath of excrement.

"How does that feel, your fineness, your princeness?" shouted Petrus.

"Maybe now you'll think twice before coming here to insult us and make fun of us!" chided Nicolas, angrily.

When they let him go, the young man scrambled to his feet as quickly as he could, wiping off some of the grime from his face until he could see, and then brushing off more from the rest of his person as well. He made a sorry sight. His porcelain-like face was nearly all black with muddy streaks. His once-elegant clothing hung dripping and disfigured, the bright blue cloak now grimy and torn.

"What was that for?" shouted Ilyan, angrily, looking right at Nicolas, as though considering him the instigator.

"Now you know what it feels like," said Nicolas, starting to feel a little of his customary remorse now that the heat of the moment had passed.

"I hadn't come here to tease you," grumbled Ilyan. "How can you call yourselves monks and attack strangers so violently? But if it's violence you want, take *this!*" With that, he shoved Nicolas backward into the pile of manure. Startled by the unexpected action, Nicolas floundered until Petrus helped him to his feet. By then, the young Slav had gone.

"Stuck-up little prude!" commented Petrus. "He's spoiled and boorish. The next time he comes around, I'll beat him black and blue—and I don't care if Father Stephanus *executes* me for it!"

"No," said Nicolas, repentant once more now that the fight had been knocked out of him. "Prince Ilyan was right. We shouldn't have attacked him. Now we'll catch it, for sure—our penance will be doubled or tripled, and we won't get out of it until Christmas!"

For the next three or four days, the young men waited for the inevitable lecture from Abbot Stephanus, followed by a further decree of punishment—but it never came. *Surely by now Prince Ilyan has reported our misconduct,* Nicolas thought.

On the fifth day following the incident, the two wayward novices received a summons from the Abbot—delivered by a smug-looking Brother John—and they trudged warily to the study. Both knew that their respective callings would be seriously questioned, that they would in all likelihood be punished for a much longer term, or that their tenure at the monastery would be abruptly terminated. When they saw Prince Ilyan standing beside Abbot Stephanus, they knew they were in for it. The Slavic prince had thoroughly cleaned himself, and wore garments that, if anything, looked even fancier than those that the two novices had ruined. He had a broad smile on his face as they entered the Abbot's study.

Abbot Stephanus came forward a few paces and then stopped almost involuntarily as the stench from Nicolas and Petrus reached his nostrils, leaving several feet between himself and the two filth-ridden young men. "I have news for you two," announced the Abbot, proudly, while waving the smell away from his nose. "Your penance is at an end."

The grin on Ilyan's face grew noticeably brighter.

"A fine has been paid on your behalf," the Abbot went on, "in the form of a considerable donation to the monastery. You still had two days to go, but now you are free. Phew! From the smell of it, I'd say it came not a day too soon. You have this young man to thank. His generosity has released you."

Nicolas felt certain that his eyes must have looked as big and round as dinner plates. Petrus likewise had his eyes open wide, his mouth gaping in sheer astonishment. Ilyan gave them only kindly smiles in return.

"Part of the Prince's bargain is that the two of you should spend the remainder of the day and one night as his guest."

"We actually get to leave the monastery? Overnight?" asked Petrus, in disbelief.

"Yes," said Stephanus. "You have been cooped up in here for far too long. It will do you both good to spend some time away. Since you are not yet bound by final vows, I have given you my permission to leave temporarily. Now don't forget to thank your benefactor."

"Thank you, Prince," said Nicolas, solemnly, hardly daring to believe in his good fortune.

"Thank you, Prince," said Petrus, and even he for once appeared repentant for having so ill-treated this noble youth.

The Prince nodded and departed. Petrus and Nicolas followed, but the Abbot pulled Nicolas aside for a private moment after the other two young men had left the room.

As soon as he had his nephew alone, Abbot Stephanus delivered a strong cuff to the back of Nicolas' head.

Nicolas cried out in pain, and looked at his uncle in surprise.

"That was for continuing to be stupid," said the Abbot, gruffly. "I know what happened out in the yard, you little idiot. You are fortunate the prince is a forgiving young man. Stop acting like Petrus and act like Nico for a change. It is time to grow up! Do you understand me?" He thrust a fat, scolding finger in his nephew's face.

Nicolas nodded, humbly.

The Abbot's stern expression melted away and he relaxed into his customary joviality. "Now go and have a good time— and behave yourself, for once."

Nicolas recognized the chariot into which Prince Ilyan now invited them. It was the one that brought the Dorius family to Sunday worship. As a guest in their house, he had apparently been permitted to borrow it, which suggested to the minds of both Nicolas and his friend that the Prince's mission had perhaps been inspired by certain others.

They spoke very little, but Ilyan's cordiality continued, even though he stood very close to the two novices. The Prince pretended to ignore the stench, for which both young men felt secretly grateful.

The first place the Prince took them was to a public Roman bath. The city of Patara boasted only a handful of such places, and the chariot stopped in front of the finest. The term "public" may have been a misnomer, for only men were allowed during the midday hours. Women were allowed use of the bath in the mornings only. The bath consisted of a series of pools filled with steaming hot water, as well as chambers of steam and tepid pools for a cool down. Attendants kept the water hot, brought towels, and served refreshments, for a fee. Here the men of the city could relax before facing the rigors of the day, or unwind after strenuous hours of work. Here political talk flourished, reputations grew or were tarnished, and the latest chariot races, gladiator bouts, and other sporting events were discussed and wagers on the same were made. The usual routine was a few minutes of sweating in one of the steam chambers, followed by immersion in a hot pool, then cooling down in a tepid pool, capped off by a brisk rubdown with a towel and anointment with perfumed oil. One normally brought towels and oil for his own use, but as the two novices had brought with them none of the customary bath equipment, Ilyan procured the needed items for them from the attendants at his own expense.

Nicolas and Petrus found it gratifying to remove their filthy robes, sweat off the worst of their remaining grime and odor, and at last plunge into clean warm water. To Nicolas, it reminded him of the cleansing from sin and the price that Jesus Christ had paid with His sacrifice of blood. To Petrus, it made him feel once again like the rich young man he had been brought up to be. Ilyan seemed content to observe the contentment of his friends.

Immersion in the water soothed Nicolas' aching, tired limbs. The last thing to touch his back had been the end of Brother John's whip. Now the pain of those wounds, which had nearly healed after nine long weeks and had grown fainter with each passing day, but which still continued to be felt, diminished considerably as the muscles in his back relaxed. He also felt relief from the bone in his left leg, which had gotten slightly dislocated after the chariot accident and now caused him to walk with a subtle limp. It seldom pained him, but he always felt it, and now that awareness, too, eased noticeably. The aches in his muscles from his daily exertions for the past weeks likewise lessened. The warm water refreshed his body as well as his soul.

Prince Ilyan joined them in the bath, after having sent a servant to a nearby laundress to have his two companions' robes cleaned. Being stripped of all clothing and finding themselves together in the water of the pool had an equalizing effect, for now they conversed freely with one another, in a manner similar to that of older men who had visited in the baths together on a daily basis for years.

"Why did you not report us?" asked Petrus, the question that Nicolas as well had been burning to ask.

"You could have had us flogged or worse," said Nicolas.

"You could have added months to our punishment," added Petrus.

"But that would not have made sense!" exclaimed Ilyan. "If I had done such a thing, you would not have been my friends. And I want to be friends with you."

"After the way we treated you?" asked Nicolas. "How can you even stand to be around us?"

"All I wanted on that day was to be friends," said Ilyan. "I am sorry my temper got the better of me, and I pushed you."

"I had it coming," said Nicolas, "just as I have had other

things coming." He rubbed the back of his head, which still throbbed a little from the Abbot's mighty cuff.

"Why would you want to be friends with a pair of disgraced would-be monks?" asked Petrus. "We are hardly fit companions for royalty."

"I am not royal," said Ilyan. "In the northern country, as in some other places, the title of prince can be a noble one as well. My brother and I are noble princes, not royal ones, although we are closely related to the royal household of Kyiv. And I believe, from what I have learned of your backgrounds, that we are placed on nearly equal footing, socially speaking. Brother Petrus, your father is a nobleman and a Magistrate, is he not? And Brother Nicolas, your father was of noble birth likewise, yes?"

Nicolas nodded. "But we are not entitled to be called 'Brother' any more than you are entitled to be called royalty. We are still a long way away from our final vows."

After the hot bath, the cool bath, the rubdown, and the anointment, the three young men dressed themselves again. Petrus and Nicolas hardly recognized their robes, which had been freshly cleaned and pressed, then dried by steam and brought back to the bath to await them by the time they emerged from the pool. Now they could not only feel clean and smell clean, but look clean as well.

Their second stop was a nearby inn, where hot, fresh platters piled high with every good thing imaginable to eat were served to all three. They ate in a private dining room. The two hungry young men, whose appetites had never been truly satisfied since that fateful morning before Easter, wolfed down their food ravenously and, at Ilyan's invitation and expense, ordered second and third helpings of everything.

After neither Nicolas nor Petrus could eat another bite, Ilyan's eyes twinkled as he made another announcement. "Now, I have a further surprise for you."

During the meal, the family chariot had been dispatched

by the young prince on another errand. Now, it drew up outside and two young women, escorted by servants, entered at the inn door. Plump, rosy-cheeked Abigail and blossoming Ana eagerly greeted the two young novices. Abigail flung herself into Petrus' arms, and the black-haired novice grabbed the girl by the waist and swung her into the air before setting her on her feet once again. Ana threw her arms around Nicolas, and her proximity recalled to his mind how pretty she had always looked to him.

"These are your true benefactresses," explained Prince Ilyan. "They persuaded me to forgive you and continue to try to make friends. They arranged with their father to loan me the chariot."

The young people passed the evening in the same private dining room where the meal had been served, which had its own fireplace and offered the opportunity to get away from the noise of the common room. As they sat and talked, Nicolas found he had a hard time keeping his eyes off Ana, the sister he had always declared would one day be the most beautiful. Her green eyes, dark curls, and smooth-complexioned face kept drawing him to steal glance after glance. Once she caught him looking at her and smiled shyly, as if to say she didn't mind his attentions at all.

To his mild irritation, however, he found that Ana addressed nearly every comment to the prince, who sat on the other side of the girl, and who conversed with her in a free, earnest, and friendly manner. Not the tone of lovers, which relieved Nicolas a little, but of good, close friends who might one day fall in love with each other. Then Nicolas chided himself for harboring resentful thoughts toward the young Slav, for not only was the attitude ungrateful, he himself had no business taking an interest in any young woman, no matter how attractive he might find her.

Abigail and Petrus, on the other hand, sat shamelessly close to each other, her soft, fair hand in his roughened, calloused one, and spoke in soft, low tones as though they had been enjoying an intimate relationship for many years. It amazed Nicolas afresh how much sheer nerve his friend still possessed, even after all of their terrible misadventures together.

Prince Ilyan had procured rooms for the night—one for the sisters and one for the young men. They were to visit together for the evening, then share a breakfast in the morning, after which the prince would take the two girls back home.

"But how did you persuade Florus to allow his daughters to come away to an inn for a night, unchaperoned?" asked Nicolas of Ilyan, when the two of them were alone in the room they were to share with Petrus. "Knowing their father, I would expect him to want to come along."

"He is out of town," said Ilyan, simply. "He is visiting his older sister Marla, who lives in a villa in the country and is very ill. While he is gone, my brother Korin and myself have been left in charge of the girls."

"Florus put your brother in charge of his own fiancee?" asked Nicolas. "Isn't that—well—sort of a dangerous thing to do, considering the wedding is still some months away?"

"He knows we are Christians," said Ilyan. "He trusts us to do the right thing."

"Does he trust you and the girls alone at an inn?" asked Nicolas.

"I never asked," laughed Ilyan. "But he need never find out about this. It was their idea, anyway. Besides, even your Abbot approved of the arrangement. The girls will behave themselves, and so will you and I."

But what about Petrus? wondered Nicolas.

As it turned out, Petrus did not come to bed that night. Not having him there worked out well for Nicolas and the prince, for they had ample room in what would have been a crowded bed had their friend been present. Despite this, Nicolas did not sleep well for worrying about what fresh mischief brewed in his absent companion's restless spirit.

He and Ilyan did not see Petrus until the next morning

when they opened the door to the corridor and found their yawning black-haired friend about to enter their bedchamber. Though he looked almost asleep, Petrus perked up when he saw the other two, and readily agreed to join them as they headed down the stairs to the private dining room, where a breakfast awaited.

Ana came in to breakfast a few minutes later, informing the young men that Abigail remained asleep.

"I'm worried," she confided to Nicolas in a whisper, as she took a few bites from her steaming plateful. "My sister hadn't come to bed yet when I fell asleep, and when I awoke this morning I could not rouse her. She is generally a healthy sleeper and an early riser."

Nicolas only nodded and remarked that he hoped Abigail was not sick. Keeping his own counsel in the matter, he could only make apprehensive surmises about what had gone on the previous night. He hoped and prayed he was wrong about his friend, but hoping and praying had not prevented calamity before.

Petrus ate his breakfast with a good appetite, and certainly seemed not to be suffering from any guilty conscience. Nicolas knew that a fine sense of honor did exist in his companion's heart, even though more primal, instinctive drives sometimes obscured the nobler motives. He also knew that Petrus was accustomed to having his own way, and had no real sense of anything being off limits. Had his friend broken any more rules, or hadn't he? Had honor and right prevailed, or had the desires of the flesh overruled propriety? Not knowing the answers caused a greater agony for Nicolas than he had known in the long weeks of penance.

After Prince Ilyan had paid the innkeeper in full, Abigail finally came down the stairs, looking as rosy-cheeked and bright-spirited as usual. But Nicolas noticed a subtle difference in her. Whereas the day before her pleasantness and joy in their company had been genuine and without affectation, today she had to force herself to display a pleasant, warm demeanor. Though outwardly she remained the same, Nicolas could tell that inwardly something was wrong. Again he prayed that his suspicions would prove entirely false.

In the days that followed, as the two novices picked up the threads of their former existence before the long punishment, Nicolas found himself and Petrus inexplicably distant from one another. The dark-haired one had grown furtive and secretive. He no longer stayed by his friend's side for hours at a time. Petrus spent, curiously enough, increased time in prayer and private meditation. When Nicolas pulled his friend aside to speak to him and find out what was wrong, Petrus insisted he was fine and refused to say anymore.

The novices had now graduated from cleaning up the worst of the filth. That task had been assigned to others who had since broken rules. Now they assisted in the stables in taking care of the horses and other animals. It represented a gigantic step up, but Petrus failed to see it that way. He complained that his clothes still reeked of the stables and the manure, even though he now was free to clean himself. He began to talk as though he were finally ready to admit his lack of a true calling to the monastic life.

Nicolas desperately wanted to have a heart-to-heart talk with his close companion, but Petrus now shut him out, speaking only as needed. This went on for a week or more, and then suddenly it was over.

Petrus' tenure with the monastery ended as abruptly as it had begun. One morning, Nicolas observed that his friend had not appeared at matins or at breakfast. Wondering if his companion were ill, the golden-haired novice went upstairs to Petrus' chamber, and found it empty. Even the good shoes had vanished.

Only later in the day did he learn what had happened. Abbot Stephanus summoned his nephew to the study and informed him that on the previous day Petrus had been caught making love to a young lady in the middle of the supposedly-empty sanctuary. Nicolas was not told the name of the young lady, but he didn't have to guess. He knew who it was. His suspicions about his friend had been correct after all. Needless to say, dismissal from the monastery would follow.

"Where is he now?" asked Nicolas, hoping at least for a chance to say goodbye.

"He is in the chapel, praying," said Stephanus. "He has gone there of his own choosing. I knew you would want to speak with him. I rather think he wants to speak to you."

Nicolas hurried to the chapel, where he found his friend kneeling, a look of anguish and repentance on the young former novice's face. Petrus still wore his black robes.

"The Reverend Father told me I have to leave," he murmured, in a stunned voice.

"You knew it was wrong," said Nicolas, tears forming in his eyes. "Why did you do it? Why?"

"The same reason I do everything, I guess," sighed Petrus. "I couldn't help myself."

"I thought you *wanted* to serve Christ. I thought you *wanted* to be a monk."

"I still do," said Petrus. "I want it more than anything. I don't want to leave, Nico."

"Why didn't you think of that before?" asked Nicolas.

"I don't know. I thought it would be like the last few times. I expected to be punished. I was ready to be punished. I didn't think he would tell me to leave." A sob burst from the former novice. He buried himself in Nicolas' arms, while Nicolas patted him on the back.

"Maybe it's for the best," murmured Nicolas. "Maybe you just aren't cut out for this way of life."

"But *you* are!" sobbed Petrus. "If you can be a monk, why can't I?"

"Because," said Nicolas. "You're not me. You'll never be me and I'll never be you. Not even in a thousand years. Don't you see? We've spent our entire lives trying to make ourselves fit into each other's mold. Yet we're still friends, even for all that. And we can go on being friends forever. It doesn't matter if I'm a monk and you're not. Just as it doesn't matter if you choose to wear fine clothes and drive around in a splendid chariot."

"I want to serve God," protested Petrus. "I love Him, and I want to serve Him."

"Maybe God wants you to serve Him by having all of those nice things and being a rich young man. He has different paths for each of us to follow."

Petrus broke away, and rubbed the tears out of his eyes. "But what can I do now? Where can I go? How can I live?"

"Why don't you marry the girl? You love her, after all. I know even your most thoughtless actions spring from love. And leaving the monastery frees you from having to take a vow of celibacy."

"I could have taken vows of celibacy and poverty," said Petrus. "I can be as strong as you can. I have just as much will-power and just as much strength of character."

"No," said Nicolas. "Don't you see? You're meant to experience the things that I am pledged to avoid. It's all right. God never meant for you to be as I am. He never meant for us to be exactly alike. You can have a wife, and raise a fine family, and still be a godly man. And I think—I think Abigail needs you just now."

Petrus gasped. "How did you know it was she?" he asked.

"I have eyes," said Nicolas. "I also know it was not the first time the two of you have been together as lovers—don't you see that sneaking around behind her father's back and behind Father Stephanus' back is *wrong?* If you and she could be honor-ably engaged, you wouldn't have to keep your love hidden any longer."

"That's true," murmured Petrus, thoughtfully.

"God will bless your union," said Nicolas. "You will be

happy with her—much happier than you could ever be behind these walls."

Petrus remained silent for several minutes as he pondered the words of his closest friend. Finally, he drew a deep breath and spoke.

"I'll miss you, Nico," he said. "If there's one thing I've enjoyed these past months, it's been your constant companionship."

"It's been the same for me, my friend," said Nicolas.

They shook hands and embraced, closer now than they had ever been. Both understood that their friendship would endure whatever path either of them took, even though regret about their parting—and the reason for it—filled them both with sorrow.

After Petrus left the monastery, Nicolas fled back to the Abbot's study, buried his head in his uncle's ample robes, and wept like a baby.

CHAPTER TWELVE:

Nico's Dream

"Nicolas!"

The dazzling brightness nearly overwhelmed his eyes. He drew closer and closer to the Throne. "Who is it that calls?" he asked. "I cannot see."

"Fear not, it is I. You have known Me since you were a child."

"Yes, Lord. What is your will?" He knelt reverently at the Throne of thrones. When he looked up, he beheld the Face, which was composed mostly of light. The Face looked down at him with compassion, with forgiveness, and with earnest exhortation.

"Take thou these robes."

Suddenly, he held the robes of a priest in one hand.

"Take thou this book of the Gospels."

The book which suddenly appeared in his other hand was covered in rubies, emeralds, and diamonds. "Lord," he asked, "Why have you given me these things?"

"Go thou, and take my gifts to the world." The Face grew bright again, and the Throne grew brighter and brighter, and the jewels on the book shone brighter as well. The brilliant light glowed and glowed until . . .

Nicolas sat up in bed. Not for the first time had he dreamed this dream. Always the same dream, down to the last detail. He pondered the message that the Lord had spoken. *Go thou, and take my gifts to the world.* What gifts could He possibly mean? And what was the significance of the priestly robes and the book? There were no books of such splendor to be found anywhere. This time the words repeated over and over in his brain. *Go thou, and take my gifts to the world. Go thou, and take my gifts to the world.*

Unable to sleep, he tossed and turned for several minutes. He had a sense that something was wrong. At length he got up from his straw mat and adjusted his robe. He padded down the stone corridors in his bare feet as quickly as his lithe and slender sixteen-year-old body could move, and made his way out to the stables.

The temperate Mediterranean climate made for a relatively warm winter's night, although a cool breeze blew. He crossed the monastery courtyard and lifted the latch to the stable door. When he entered, he sensed why he had been drawn to this place at this hour. The white horse neighed and whinnied in a disturbed, restless kind of way.

Nicolas got along well in the stables, in fact much better than he had in the kitchen. The animals liked him and Brother Marcus, who was in charge of the livestock, liked him as well. Although he found the work tiring, he also found it to be extremely agreeable and now that he had no built-in distraction of trying to mentor his best friend, he could concentrate much better on his duties.

In addition to his work in the stables, Nicolas was reinstated as Head Novice, and every new applicant became his responsibility. Since the disaster of his previous experience, he had learned much about leadership and working with others. While he took every interest in the welfare of his charges, he took care not to get too close to any of them. The youngest ones in particular looked upon him as a big brother, and he did his best to keep them at arm's length, giving them only the smallest amount of nurturing and constantly encouraging them to do for themselves all the things they wanted him to do for them. It was a long way to have come in a matter of months.

"There, there," he comforted the horse, patting its long, white neck. "I can't sleep, either." He did his best to soothe the restless beast, but soon realized that the animal had gotten too restive to settle down easily. He tried to think how long it had been since the horse had been exercised, but realized it had only been the previous afternoon. The horse should have been able to make it through the night.

No matter what he did, the horse would not calm down. There was nothing else to do but to take it for an airing. He lifted the saddle down from where it hung on the wall, and prepared the animal for riding. He also unearthed a warm cloak and a pair of dry, sturdy boots.

It would be several hours yet before matins. He could easily have the animal back in the stable by then. Brother Marcus would understand about Nicolas' temporary absence, for the stable master had sometimes had to do this very thing himself.

When he and the stallion were properly outfitted, Nicolas mounted the steed and rode out of the enclosure and into the streets of Patara. *Cadeau*. That was what Brother Arvix from Gaul had named the creature. *Cadeau. Gift. Bring my gifts to the world* . . . Nicolas' cloak whipped behind him as he rode the white horse through the streets of the city.

Of late, terrible times had befallen Patara, indeed all of Lycia. An economic downturn spurred by a poor agricultural season, a harvest virtually wiped out by devastating storms, rampant inflation, and an increase in import and export taxes brought about by a new imperial administration had threatened the well-being of every citizen in the Mediterranean port town. The same storm that had destroyed crops and livestock in October had also wrecked several prominent buildings and homes in the city as well. Those who had previously prospered now suffered from reduced income, loss of home and other possessions, and lack of available work.

More and more people turned to the church to take care of their needs, but even the resources of the monastery and the convent reached a limit after awhile, and the soups and breads offered to help line the stomachs of the poor became watered-down and doughy. Those who proved best able to cope were the monks and the nuns, who were used to living without luxuries or much food, and so didn't feel the pangs of starvation as greatly as those who had been accustomed to more. To all intents and purposes, the church seemed alive and well, although the rumors from Rome were that Diocletian, the new Emperor, had an anti-Christian agenda and desired to encourage the worship of the old Roman gods. The church had much to worry about in these times, as if the possibility of financial ruin was not grievous enough.

The only ones whose fortunes didn't suffer were those whose wealth had been sufficiently great at the start and who were thus able to sustain the losses incurred by hard times. Nicolas' own personal fortune actually grew during this time and this embarrassed him greatly. He chose never to speak of his wealth to anyone, but he resolved afresh to do everything in his power to help those in need.

It was now December and plans had been laid for an elaborate New Year's wedding to celebrate the marriage of Prince Korin Koratovich to Angelina, daughter of the nobleman Florus Dorius. Abbot Stephanus and the holy brothers had been involved in the preparations, as their chapel had been designated as the place where the wedding would be held. The Abbot himself had planned to perform the ceremony. A frenzy of excitement had been built up in anticipation of the great event.

Suddenly, everything had stopped. The wedding had been canceled and Prince Korin and his brother had returned to the northern country. The reason? Nobody knew. Nicolas suspected that an argument might have been the cause of the rift, but it remained guesswork. Florus and his daughters also had stopped attending worship.

Nicolas felt very sorry, and not just for the bride and groom and their respective families. He grieved because now things didn't look good for Petrus. The black-haired young man had proposed to his beloved Abigail, and she had accepted. Young Maximus had also won the father's approval and consent. The wedding date had been set for the following year, a few months after Angelina's marriage. Now Nicolas feared that the present crisis might jeopardize Petrus' future happiness.

As Cadeau bore him through the streets of Patara, Nicolas found himself in a district he did not recognize. The modest home where his parents had lived lay on the other side of town. Senator Maximus' imposing dwelling stood at the opposite end. The only person he knew who lived in the central part of town was Florus, and the street down which the stallion now cantered did not lead in the direction of that family's palatial villa. He wondered why the horse had chosen this particular direction for his nighttime walk. Nicolas had allowed Cadeau to take his own way, figuring that sooner or later the beast would tire sufficiently to consider returning home to its stable.

Yet the white stallion seemed to be on a mission. It was determined to go in a certain direction, and even when Nicolas tired of the ride and wanted to go back to the monastery, he could not persuade Cadeau to abandon the present course. The creature continued to wend its way through the nearly empty streets. At length, the animal stopped. Nicolas dismounted, to give the horse a chance to regain its breath. The horse nickered and nudged the novice affectionately, as if showing its appreciation for understanding the need for the ride.

However, now, as he made ready to remount, Nicolas found that the horse still refused to leave him alone. It continued to nudge and press the young man until Nicolas found himself right against the side of a nearby dwelling. It was a shabby, run-down house in a disreputable part of town. Nicolas didn't want to stay there any longer than he could help, but now that the horse had gently but firmly pressed him to the wall, he heard the sound of voices coming from a nearby window. Familiar voices, too.

"We have no other choice."

"No, there is always another way."

"Sister, we have no money. Father is too sick with grief to do anything. We will starve or die."

"She's right, little one. Ever since Aunt Marla passed away in the fall, Father has not been himself. And then to lose our house . . . it was more than he could stand."

"I can go to work. I'm young and strong, and I don't mind working hard. I will take care of the family, if I must. Only don't do that . . . don't even consider it . . ."

"There is no work. You surely know that. That is why so many are starving and suffering."

Nicolas peered through a crack in the wooden shutter. The sight inside confirmed what he had feared from the snatch of conversation he had overheard. The voices had indeed been those of Angelina, Abigail, and Ana. Florus' three daughters sat close to a small fire in the hearth of this humble dwelling, talking over their troubles. In front of the blaze their white wolfhound lay dozing with one eye open. It filled Nicolas with sorrow to see these sisters, who had always had servants to wait on them, reduced to washing their own stockings in a basin and hanging them over the fire to dry.

"I blame Korin for our difficulties," pouted Abigail. "If he had only been man enough to marry you no matter what, we wouldn't be living like this now."

"It wasn't his fault," said Angelina. "He couldn't marry me if I had no dowry. His family would not allow it."

"And he couldn't have loaned you the money?"

"I wouldn't have taken it," said Angelina proudly. "Anyway, his family is not much better off than we are since the past autumn, as trade in Novgorod has been greatly affected. I didn't blame him for leaving. What choice did he have? He and his brother couldn't rely on our hospitality any longer, and

Korin didn't want to inconvenience us in any way." She patted the wolfhound, which had moved from one side of the hearth to the other and now settled down as the eldest sister patted his head and scratched his ears.

"I have it!" exclaimed Abigail, her eyes momentarily brightening. "I'll ask Petrus Maximus for a loan. He is rich enough to finance *two* weddings! Then Korin can come back and marry you, and Petrus and I can be married afterward!"

Angelina shook her head sadly. "Haven't you heard?" she asked. "The Maximus family has lost their fortune, likewise. It is rumored that Petrus and his father are about to sell their house and move into small, modest quarters in another part of town. They say the pressures have driven the father nearly mad."

"Poor Petrus," sighed Abigail. "Caring for a lunatic father in a set of small rooms when he has been used to so much finery—no wonder I have not seen him for months. It's got to be difficult for him."

"We must face the cold, hard truth, girls," said Angelina. "The only way for us to have the kind of life we are used to is to marry. We can never marry without sufficient dowries, which we do not have. If we do not marry, we must work to earn money to feed and clothe ourselves. There is no work, so we cannot earn money that way. There is only one way left to earn money that I can think of, and that is—"

"No!" exclaimed Ana, in horror. "Oh, no, no! Do not say it! Do not think it! It is wicked!" Finishing hanging up a stocking, she then went to the dog and buried her face in its warm fur, thus muffling her cries of grief.

"What choice have we?" asked Angelina, with a sigh. "Now, don't worry, Ana and Abigail. Neither of you is fully developed yet. I—have a womanly figure, and I am full grown. I will take it upon myself to—"

"Wait, at least," pleaded Ana. "Give me a chance to pray first. I will pray for God to send us a miracle."

"Child," said Angelina, "all of us been praying for many months, to no avail. The situation is hopeless."

"Give it just a few more days," begged Ana.

"Very well," said Angelina. "We have enough food to last us until Christmas, which is twelve days away. Unless one of your prayers gets answered before then, I will have to earn us some money in whatever way I can."

Nicolas shuddered with revulsion at the thought of the sacrifice the eldest daughter was willing to make. She was the one whom he had always considered to be aloof and remote. He found it touching that she tried so hard to make the girls' well-being her responsibility and hers alone. He had a newfound respect for her, in spite of or perhaps because of her grim resolution.

Now the other daughters had left the room. He heard the youngest as she stood by the window to pray her special prayer. By the closeness of her voice, she was right on the other side of the wooden shutter. He could have reached forward and grasped her by the hand. For a moment, he came near to doing just that, and to assuring her that he had enough money to help them. However, he rejected the notion as soon as it occurred to him. The girls had too much pride. They wouldn't accept help of that kind, even from a family friend. Then a plan began to form in his mind.

"Blessed Jesus," prayed Ana, "send one of your good angels to come help us in our time of need. Please grant us money for the dowries we need to marry, and please put food on our table, and give us enough clothes to wear. Help us to keep a roof over our heads. Bless my sisters and our father, and protect us and take care of us, and keep us warm and safe."

At that moment, Nicolas understood the words of his dream. *Go thou, and take my gifts to the world.* So this was God's purpose in bringing him here tonight! He would never have found the house on his own. He would never have known of the Dorius girls' plight. And he would never have thought of the wonderful plan he had now conceived.

The horse had been given plenty of time to catch its breath. It now appeared ready for him to mount. Inside the house the dog gave a low growl, as though sensing the presence of an intruder nearby, so the young man knew it was time to move. While little Ana continued to murmur her prayers on the other side of the shuttered window, Nicolas, as soundlessly as possible, got astride the horse and rode off through the streets of Patara. He didn't need to worry that they might have gotten lost. The horse had led him straight here, and Nicolas felt certain that the animal would have no difficulty in bringing them both safely back to the monastery.

CHAPTER THIRTEEN:

The First Christmas Gift

"Father, I ask your permission to absent myself from the Christmas Eve midnight mass," said Nicolas.

"And what is your reason for such a request, Head Novice?" asked the Abbot.

They hardly ever called each other uncle and nephew any more. The terms between them had grown more formal as Nicolas' commitment to his calling deepened. More and more, Stephanus had become the Reverend Father to his late brother's son, because it was in that capacity that the young man now needed the older man's guidance. While their love for one another remained as strong as ever, their relations toward each other had altered subtly in the last months. Except for the fact that his uncle never could look on him as a stranger, Nicolas had become more like just another member of the order.

"I have business . . . the Lord's business," explained the Head Novice.

Abbot Stephanus looked Nicolas over carefully. "All right, Nico," he said, after having given considerable thought to the matter. "You have my leave to miss the midnight mass . . . but you must promise to be present for morning prayers on Christmas day."

"Yes, Father," said Nicolas.

"You ruined Easter . . . I hope you're not planning on ruining Christmas, too."

"No, sir. I learned my lesson then. I would not ask this if I did not sense God's will at work."

The older man smiled. "Several months ago, I told you to grow up. It looks as though you have."

"I have, Father," said Nicolas, earnestly.

"You've gotten taller . . . your voice has stopped squeaking . . . your limbs are gradually becoming more proportionate . . . I would say you've done a fine job of growing up, inside and out."

"Thank you, Father." A faint smile played across Nicolas' lips.

Getting the money proved to be a more difficult matter than expected. Nicolas found he could not withdraw on the principal balance until he reached the age of twenty-four years. In the meantime, the funds were kept in a trust managed by his late father's accountant, who did not regard seriously the young man's intent to take his monastic vows in another year's time. The accountant, an Arabian named Ahmed, considered the matter a young man's passing fancy, nothing more nor less, and informed the sixteen-year-old that the money would remain in the trust indefinitely if not claimed by the age of majority.

"How much may I take right now?" asked Nicolas, earnestly.

"You may touch only the interest that has not yet been added to the principal," said Ahmed the accountant.

"And that is how much?" asked Nicolas.

"The interest remains fixed at its current rate," said the accountant, avoiding a direct answer, "so it will be best for you to touch none of the money before your twenty-fourth birthday."

"I need about thirty gold pieces," said Nicolas.

"Why?" asked the accountant. "Are you planning to get married?"

"No," said the young novice in amusement, "but someone is."

He had to sign his name to a few pieces of paper before

the accountant would give him any money, but eventually he had the thirty gold pieces in a sack. The gold pieces felt heavy when he tied the sack to the inside of his robe. It amused him to recall how he would have considered such a sum paltry in his childhood, when he had thought nothing of spending money as though it were water and had no idea of its real value. Why, he had even wagered a *thousand* gold pieces on the outcome of that foolish chariot race!

On Christmas Eve, while the holy brothers prepared for the mass, Nicolas went to the stable, where Brother Marcus awaited him. Cadeau was saddled and ready.

"Thank you, Brother Marcus," said Nicolas, putting on the boots and the warm cloak that the monk held out for him. "It was good of you to grant me permission to take the white stallion."

"Cadeau often needs a good scamper at night like this," said Brother Marcus. "But I must say, Novice Nicolas, you're being awfully mysterious about this errand of yours."

"It's a merciful errand, Brother, and a godly one, I hope." He put a hand to his waist to stop the bag of money from jingling.

"I hope so, too," said Brother Marcus, whose ears had pricked up at the sound of coins clinking together.

"Merry Christmas, Brother Marcus."

"Merry Christmas, Nico. May God bless you, whatever you're up to."

More of a bustle than usual could be observed in the city streets as the faithful wended their way to the services to celebrate the birth of Christ. It surprised Nicolas how many believers there were, considering the number of pagans and followers of other faiths that lived in Patara. Yet the religion of Christ always seemed to attract goodly numbers into its folds, a fact Nicolas attributed to the potency of its simple message.

He caught a glimpse of one man's face in the light of a torch that flickered on the side of the street, and found it to be someone he recognized. It was Enu, the shepherd, who had been taking his sheep to market on the day of the catastrophic chariot race. Having no clear recollection of the accident itself, and having been knocked unconscious at the scene, he remembered the old man from the days following, when Enu had tried to extract money from Ephanus to compensate for the loss of several of his sheep. The old man had trembled violently then, and he did so now, the trembling apparently having been brought on by the trauma of the accident.

"Pardon me, holy brother," muttered the old man as he brushed past Nicolas' horse.

"Enu?" asked Nicolas, looking into the shepherd's face.

"That's my name, holy brother. Now how would you happen to know me?" Clearly, the old shepherd did not recognize Nicolas, who had grown up considerably since that day.

"I met you long ago," said Nicolas. "You probably don't remember me. I never thought I would see you on your way to a church."

"Well, you see," said Enu, trembling worse than ever, "I were in a turrible accident several years back. An' I might have died. But I lived, you see, I lived. And though it didn't occur to me at first, I realized as time passed that I ought to be thankful to God for savin' my life. So I turned to God shortly after, an' I've been turnin' to Him ever since. I've never stopped atremblin' since that accident, but I bless it all the same, yes, I bless it, because it put me on the path to God." He grinned a wide, nearly toothless grin, then paused and looked closely into Nicolas' face. "Oughtn't I to know you, holy brother? You look mighty familiar."

"I don't think so," said Nicolas, discreetly. "As I said, it was a long time ago, and you have doubtless forgotten me."

The old man nodded and went on his way to worship.

Nicolas pondered the vagaries of life. *That chariot race was one of the most foolish things I ever got involved in,* he mused, *yet God used it to bring that sheep farmer to Him.* He also thought of the humble shepherds who nearly three hundred years earlier had been keeping watch over their flocks by night when they were visited by the angel and the Heavenly Host. God had used them to spread the news of Jesus' birth. *I hope that God will someday use me as He used those humble shepherds to bring others to Him.*

In the clear sky above, a single star shone brighter than the others. According to the lessons Brother Augustus had taught him, it was Venus, the morning star, which he now beheld. But Nicolas pretended that it was the same star that had guided the wise men to the lowly place where the infant Jesus had lived. Like Nicolas, they had brought gifts to the poor, with their presents of gold, frankincense, and myrrh. Perhaps they, too, had been directed by God to give His gifts. Perhaps this star would serve as Nicolas' own guide, and would lead him to the humble abode he now sought, just as the other star had done for those long-ago seekers of Christ.

Nicolas had no idea where the house stood. That first night, they had twisted and turned down so many side streets he couldn't have begun to find it again on his own. He trusted Cadeau to take him right to it, as the horse had done the other night. So far, the stallion seemed to know exactly which streets to follow and they moved along at a steady pace.

After awhile, the horse reached the humble abode where Florus and his three daughters now lived. As he rode up, Nicolas reflected on how the Christ child had likewise been born in humble circumstances. He imagined that this home was like the stable in which Mary, His mother, had first laid the infant Jesus down to sleep in the hay, while Joseph, His father, stood guard over those precious charges. They had traveled many miles to Bethlehem for the census, while Mary was carrying Our Savior in her womb, and the birth pangs had come upon her before they had even found a place to stay. As the inns were crowded, a stable had been their only place of refuge. Some traditions even said it had been a cave. Despite the rude and unworthy accommodations, the miracle of Jesus' birth had occurred to bring joy and blessings to his parents, and eventually to the entire world as the ultimate gift from God. As with the family that Nicolas now visited, God had seen fit to bless those in reduced circumstances.

Tethering his steed to a nearby post, Nicolas told Cadeau to wait quietly. The horse nodded.

Nicolas crept to the window where he had listened to Ana's prayer. As before, it stood shuttered but unlocked. He drew back the shutter for a look inside, but instantly pulled back. Ana stood holding a candle in the center of the room. Through the crack in the shutter, he watched her as she approached the window again and prayed.

"O, Blessed Jesus, let your angel come tonight!" she exclaimed, in a voice that expressed a kind of disappointed hope, as though she sensed that what she asked might not come to pass.

The angel is here, child. Just go to bed and your troubles will be at an end. He wished she would go to bed. She seemed to linger at the window for the longest time. As he crouched underneath the sill, with her tearful, pleading face just inches above his, he longed to hold her and caress her, and to tell her that everything would be all right, but he could not do any such thing without giving the whole plan away.

After several minutes, she moved away from the spot where she had been standing and patted the wolfhound, which lay snoozing by the fire. At her bidding, the dog readily followed her into her bedchamber, or so Nicolas assumed when he saw the animal go with her.

At last, when all had fallen still, Nicolas slowly pulled open the window shutter and climbed inside the house. He closed the shutter behind him but did not latch it. The modest little room contained very little furniture—a few chairs, a couple of stools, and a table. The only light came from the stars and moon shining in through the window, and the faint glow of the smoldering fire. His eyes cast about for a suitable place to hide a treasure. It had to be a place where the girls would be sure to look, yet it shouldn't be too obvious. He thought of placing the sack under one of the stools, but he feared the dog might get to it first. There had to be a place where the girls would find it, yet which the dog couldn't reach. Then his eyes fell on the stockings. The sisters had hung their stockings over the fireplace to dry. There would be enough room inside one stocking for the sack with the thirty gold pieces, although it would stretch the garment considerably. It was certainly an odd place to hide money, but it seemed to be the best choice. So Nicolas stuffed the bag of coins into one of the longest stockings, which he felt certain had to belong to the older sister. Breathing a sigh of relief, he turned to head back toward the window, when his escape was momentarily arrested by a low growl.

"R-r-r-r-r-r-r-r," growled the wolfhound, which Nicolas thought Ana had taken into her room. The dog stood menacingly at his feet, as though daring him to take a step forward. The young novice tried to make a run for the window, but at his first movement, the dog barked.

"Boris? Boris!" came the cry from the youngest sister. A moment later, she came out, carrying a candle for light. Nicolas tried to squeeze himself into the shadows and dared not even breathe.

"Woof! Woof!" barked Boris, trying hard to get his mistress' attention.

"Naughty, naughty dog," scolded Ana. "Mustn't bark and wake everyone." She spanked the wolfhound with the back of her hand. "No!"

Punished for barking, the dog reverted to the low growl, keeping a steady focus on Nicolas. The young man pressed himself against the wall.

Ana held her candle up and down and moved it all around. For an instant, the light caught a part of Nicolas' black robe, but the robe merely blended into the darkness, so Ana did not notice it. After she had moved the light around the room a few times, but always just out of range of Nicolas, she scolded the dog again. "Naughty dog! There's nobody in here! Now come with me!" She took the dog out of the room once more, while the animal continued its steady growling at the intruder that its mistress could not see.

The moment she had disappeared into her bedchamber, the novice ran to the window, jumped out, and refastened the shutter. In next to no time, he had untied the horse, remounted, and started the long ride back to the monastery.

Arriving at the stable, he fed Cadeau and gave the horse a good rubdown and brushing before turning in. He hung up the cloak, removed the boots, and then walked across the courtyard and up the stairs to the novices' quarters. He had no trouble falling asleep.

"Nicolas. Fear not. It is I. You have known Me since you were a child. Take thou these robes. Take thou this book of Gospels. Go thou, and give my gifts to the world."

The dream startled him into wakefulness. The same dream. Why would he have it now—now that he had begun to distribute his wealth among the needy of the world? Was he not doing as the Lord had directed in the dream? Perhaps there was a greater meaning that he had failed to grasp. He resolved to tell Father Stephanus of it that very day.

CHAPTER FOURTEEN:

Nico's Dilemma

Christmas morning dawned clear and bright, the air crisp and cool. After attending to his stable duties — Brother Marcus always said that the animals' needs must be met before their own — Nicolas filed into the morning prayer session with a glad heart, thinking of the joy the girls must surely feel by now. He wanted to tell someone of what he had done, but he did not want to appear boastful, and, he reflected, *a secret is no secret if it is told.* So he contented himself with picturing in his mind the look on Angelina's face as she lifted down her stocking and found it filled with gold pieces!

As he walked out of the chapel, a hand grasped the sleeve of his robe. He found himself looking into the bright, cheerful face of Prince Ilyan Koratovich. "Prince Ilyan!" he exclaimed.

"No, Nicolas. Friends we are, you and I. I am not a prince to you. To you I am just Ilyan."

"Very well, Ilyan. What brings you here on Christmas morning? I thought you and your brother had returned to Novgorod."

"My brother and I, we had a disagreement," explained Ilyan. "After our gracious host lost his fortune, we had different ideas of the honorable thing to do. He did not want to be a burden to Florus, and since he could not marry the girl he loved without a proper dowry — our family has forbidden either of us to marry otherwise — he chose to go home to the northern coun-

169

try. I, on the other hand, felt we should stay and try to help our friends. So, though I set out to accompany my brother on the journey home, I decided at the last to remain. Besides, I like your Mediterranean climate here in Lycia. In Novgorod this time of year we would be knee-deep in snow. I am staying at the inn, the same inn where we all stayed on the night after your punishment. By the way, I hear that Petrus has left the monastery and is going to marry Abigail."

Nicolas shook his head. "No, those plans are off. Petrus must look after his father, who has also lost his fortune. I don't think Abigail would want to marry, anyway, until her elder sister is wed."

"That is what I have come to see you about," said Ilyan. "I hoped that you and I could devise some sort of plan to make the wedding between my brother and Florus' daughter possible. I know that you are a poor novice with no money, but you can speak to God, yes? You also have a good brain, better than mine. You could think of something, no?"

"Why is it so important to you?" asked Nicolas.

Ilyan grinned. "Because I care about my brother. Because he truly loves Angelina and wants what is best for her. And because — well, I am in love, too."

At that moment, Nicolas felt as though he had been stabbed in the heart. His cheerful disposition vanished in an instant. He looked at the floor and pulled his hood over his head so that most of his face hid in the shadow.

"I am in love with the youngest daughter, Ana," said Ilyan, with the earnestness of a friend sharing his inmost secrets with a close companion. "I know I am still young, but I wish to marry her as soon as possible. And if Angelina marries, then Abigail, well, Ana will be the next and last."

Swallowing hard, nearly choking on his words, Nicolas asked, "And does she — does she love you in return?"

Ilyan considered for a moment. "I think so. I truly think

so. I also do not believe she quite knows what it is to be in love yet. But, yes, I think we are falling in love together."

"God has blessed you richly," stated Nicolas, in a hollow tone.

"I know that you are going to be a monk, and you are beyond falling in love with a woman, but as for I, I cannot help myself. This Ana, I think she is the loveliest, most enchanting person on this earth. When she looks at me with her beautiful green eyes, it is like—like paradise! Of course, you have a much greater, holier love—the love of God. And that is the greatest love of all, much more fulfilling than an earthly love, yes?"

"Yes," murmured Nicolas, sadly, his eyes fixed on a tiny patch of moisture that had just dropped onto the stone floor.

"Then you will help me, my friend? You will think of a way to make it possible for Angelina, then Abigail, then Ana to marry?"

Nicolas nodded. "I have already thought of a way," he said dully, slowly. "Let us kneel and pray."

"Right here in the corridor?"

"God can hear us anywhere."

Ilyan knelt down beside the young novice. Nicolas offered up a few hollow words that utterly lacked sincerity, yet which revealed his knowledge that the answer to his prayer for a miracle for the Dorius family would be definite and certain. Then he told his friend to rise.

"Go to the house where Florus and his daughters now live." The vagueness of his directions gave no indication that he knew exactly where the house stood, but they provided enough information that Nicolas felt certain the young Slav could find it. "See if our prayer has been answered. That is the most I can do for you."

"Thank you, my friend," said Ilyan, warmly. "I know you have my best interests at heart."

"Yes," said Nicolas. "God knows what is best for us all."

After his Slavic friend had gone, Nicolas returned to the chapel. He felt a need for more prayer. His heart had grown heavy. He had to admit to himself a terrible truth — *he had fallen in love with Ana.* Knowing this made him realize that his entire career now stood on shaky ground, for a holy brother was not to be in love with anyone but the Lord. He could have endured it if she were to have renounced physical passion, as he thought he had done, and the two of them could exist together as celibates, each to his or her own separate calling, in the world yet not of the world. But to think that she might marry — and his earnest young Slavic friend was clearly sincere in his affections for the girl — was more than he could tolerate.

Where, he wondered, did his responsibilities and duties lie? Did he have an obligation to leave the church and marry the girl, as he had so strongly urged Petrus to do? Or did he have to swallow up his feelings, deny his passion, and continue on his present course, forsaking all worldly loves? Neither seemed satisfactory to him. It was like having an itch and being unable to reach it to relieve it.

He knelt in prayer. After some moments of remaining in a kneeling position, his eyes grew heavy and his wits wandered. Overcome by fatigue from his exertions of the night before, Nicolas fell asleep in the chapel.

A large, gentle hand shook him awake. "Come, come, the chapel is not a bedchamber," said Father Stephanus.

Nicolas rubbed his eyes and stood up. "Forgive me, Father," he said, solemnly.

The Abbot ushered his nephew into the study. He poured a glass of wine for each of them, in celebration of the holiday. "Tell me, Nico, did you accomplish your — business last night?"

"Yes, Father Stephanus," said Nicolas.

"You appear troubled. Did it not work out all right?"

"No, Father," said Nicolas. "I mean, yes, Father. It all fell into place, just as I imagine the Lord wanted it to."

"Tell me what it is that is troubling you."

He didn't dare tell about Ana. Not until he had reached a decision of his own about the matter. So instead he related the other problem that troubled him—his recurring dream.

"What can it mean, Father?" asked Nicolas.

"I will tell you what I think, Head Novice," began the Abbot.

Just then a brother interrupted with word that a young man anxiously wanted to see Abbot Stephanus. A moment later, Prince Ilyan pranced exuberantly into the study. His hat had fallen off his head, his reddish-brown hair stuck out in all directions, and he seemed out of breath.

"Father Stephanus! Nico! The prayer worked! It is a miracle!"

"Calm down, Prince," said Stephanus, pouring a glass of wine for the young man and bidding him to be seated. "Let us drink to your good health." He raised his glass. Nicolas and Ilyan did the same. "A merry Christmas to you, sir!" exclaimed the Abbot.

"And a merry Christmas to both of you, likewise," said Ilyan. "I have just come from the house of Florus and his daughters. Nico, you will never guess what has happened!"

"We won't guess if you don't tell us," said the Abbot, with a twinkle in his eye.

"Angelina hung her stockings by the fireplace to dry, last evening before she went to bed. When she took them down this morning, she found a bag of gold in one of them—enough for a dowry and to pay the family's expenses for a long time to come!"

"It *is* a miracle!" exclaimed the Abbot.

"God works in mysterious ways," said Nicolas, furtively. "Then the wedding is on?"

"Yes," said Ilyan. "Or, it will be as soon as word can be brought to my brother. I shall leave for Novgorod this day to fetch him!"

The young Slav embraced the novice. "My friend, it was

your prayer that did it! You have made it possible for all of our dreams to come true! First, Angelina. Next, Abigail. Then, it will be Ana's turn, and I shall be the happiest man alive! Oh, Nicolas, you can never know how much I love her!"

"Yes, I can imagine," murmured Nicolas.

"And I love you for bringing it to pass!" Ilyan embraced his friend and kissed Nicolas on either cheek. "You have been more than a friend, Nicolas, and I will never forget it!"

With that, the prince dashed out of the study, and made ready for the journey to the northern country.

The Abbot looked carefully at his nephew. "I wonder how that money got into that stocking?"

"How should I know?" asked Nicolas, miserably. "I can't see how I could possibly have had anything to do with it."

Stephanus reached out and put a hand on his nephew's knee. "So that was your Lord's business last night. It was a generous and noble thing to do, Nico, and I am proud of you. I think God is proud of you, too."

"Then why am I still having that dream? I dreamed it again just now in the chapel. What is the dream, Father? The priestly robes and the book of Gospels? The admonition to give God's gifts to the world. What does it mean?"

"I think it means, Nico, that you are no longer fit to become a monk."

Nicolas gasped. "No, Reverend Father! It can't mean that! It can't! This is my life! This is where I belong!" He thought it was all over. He thought that somehow his love for Ana had been represented in the dream, that the Abbot had guessed about his passion, and that soon Nicolas would be leaving the monastery in disgrace as Petrus had.

"Let me finish. As I was saying, it means," the Abbot pronounced, "that instead you are to become a priest."

CHAPTER FIFTEEN:

A Friend in Need

The wedding of Prince Korin Koratovich and Angelina Doria, daughter of Florus, finally took place in May, in the chapel of the monastery. Abbot Stephanus officiated. In attendance were the monks and novices and members of both families, including Abigail and Ana, Florus, Prince Ilyan, and even the wolfhound, who stood tied up just outside the chapel door. The only persons noticeably absent were Petrus Maximus and his father, the former Senator.

The marriage ceremony had been delayed five months from its original date, for cold winds and blizzards in Novgorod had made travel difficult, and it had taken more weeks than anticipated for Prince Ilyan to bring the good news and fetch his brother from up north. A pleasure deferred is sometimes all the sweeter for the waiting, so the festivities were celebrated with great rejoicing.

The Prince stood tall and proud, his expression solemn and undecipherable as usual. The bride wore a gown of sky blue and an indigo cloak with gold trim. Nicolas thought she had never looked lovelier. The other two girls, likewise, wore fine new gowns and looked like princesses. The young novice could not help feeling a pang in his heart every time he looked at the pretty, green-eyed youngest daughter. He noticed that Ilyan's eyes remained on Ana during the entire ceremony.

The fact that his oldest and closest friend had not

appeared at the wedding filled Nicolas' heart with unease. After all, the marriage of Angelina paved the way for Petrus' marriage to Abigail. The young novice felt that something must be wrong for his friend to have stayed away. He therefore asked leave, on the day after the wedding, to call on the Maximus family.

The great house stood nearly empty. The entry hall and dining room were bare of furniture. No servants bustled about, preparing meals or baths or readying the horses or the chariots. Eerie echoes filled the vast chambers as Nicolas made his way to his friend's room. Even that stood empty.

Memories filled his mind of the days when he had lived here and tried so hard to become a part of the Maximus family's lifestyle of wealth and splendor—such desires seemed foreign to him now. Here in this very house had also been the beginning of his education. It was here that he had first learned some cold, hard truths about money and possessions. It was here also that he had first encountered, through his prayers, the person of Christ. As he gazed through the corridors and the bare rooms, he felt amazed at how far he had since traveled on his spiritual journey. The boy he had once been now seemed a mere shadow of the man he had become.

There seemed to be nobody about. He examined empty room after empty room. After a few minutes, he heard movement behind one of the doors. Opening the door slightly, he peered inside the room. A wild-eyed Sergius Maximus grabbed him by the tunic and shook him until his teeth rattled. "It's about time you came!" he roared. "I've been yelling for you for an hour! Where's my wine? What have you done with it?" He raised his walking stick, about to deliver a blow.

"Stop it, Papa! Stop it!" shouted Petrus, who now came running, pale and out of breath, into the room. He grabbed the old man's arm and held it firmly, preventing the stick from descending onto Nicolas' head. Beads of sweat poured down the dark-haired young man's brow. "This isn't a servant. This is Nico. You remember. You used to say you liked him when he was a little boy."

A confused look crept over the old man's face. Lowering his walking stick, he narrowed his eyes and turned his head as he scrutinized the newcomer, apparently trying without success to recall the face. "Nico," he repeated, slowly. "Nico. Ni-co."

"Papa's not quite himself today," apologized Petrus. "He has his better days and worse days. Sometimes he doesn't even know who I am."

"Petrus . . . your clothes . . . your shoes . . . your cloak . . ." murmured Nicolas.

"I got accustomed to poverty when I was trying to become a monk," said Petrus, trying valiantly to assume an air of bravado. "I've had to make do with whatever old clothes I could find. My good clothing has all been sold, or traded for food."

"A monk," repeated Sergius, as though trying to remember what the word meant.

"Papa, sit down," urged Petrus, taking the old man by the elbow and guiding him to a chair.

"Sit—sit down? What's down? Oh, down. Yes, that's it. Down. I remember." Slowly the old man sank into the chair. His head sank forward onto his chest, and he slept.

"How long has he been like this?" asked Nicolas.

"Since we lost everything," answered Petrus. "But really, it's been coming on ever since Mama died. I think he's been eaten up with guilt all these years. He didn't treat her very well and I know he cheated on her. I suspect he used to beat her occasionally, the way he used to beat me. It looks like the guilt has so tortured him that it's chipped away at his reason. Now he never knows what day it is or what time it is. He thinks we still have servants and slaves. His mind won't accept that we're no longer rich."

"Poor man!" exclaimed Nicolas, compassionately. "It must be dreadful for you."

"He's not very good company," admitted Petrus, "but then, he never was, even in his right mind. If he ever even had a right mind."

"I heard you were selling this house," said Nicolas.

Petrus shook his head. "I can't. No one will buy it. Nobody has money anymore."

"What will you do?" asked Nicolas.

Petrus sighed. "I don't know."

A snore suddenly erupted from the chair where Sergius sat. "Let's get out of this room," said Petrus.

"Shouldn't we—wouldn't he be more comfortable lying down?"

"He sleeps more soundly in that chair than anywhere else." Petrus led his friend into the room that had once been Nicolas' own. The beautiful bed with the silk sheets and satin pillows was gone. The patterned window curtains had been taken down, and nothing else had replaced them, so the window with its view of the courtyard was stark and bare. A three-legged wooden stool lay on its side near the doorway. Petrus righted it and invited Nicolas to sit down. "Where will you sit?" asked Nicolas, politely.

Petrus smirked. "I will lean, or sit on the floor. I don't much care." He plopped himself down at his friend's feet with his back against one of the walls. "Tell me, Nico, what brings you to these dismal surroundings? Does not the monastery offer enough poverty of its own, that you come to partake of mine?"

"I have been concerned about you," said Nicolas, honestly. "You didn't come to Angelina's wedding."

Petrus shrugged. "I didn't want anyone, especially Abigail, to see me like this."

"You still plan to marry Abigail, don't you?"

"Abigail is a well-brought-up young lady," said Petrus. "She is accustomed to living comfortably."

"Not anymore," said Nicolas. "You should see the house where her family lives now."

"That is not the point," said Petrus. "A girl from a good family can't be expected to marry a man who has nothing. And that's just what I am. A man who has nothing. Nothing to offer but empty rooms, a lunatic father, and an inability to keep even myself properly fed. I can't ask her to share this kind of life. I can hardly bear to live this way myself."

Nicolas nodded. "I have reason to believe," he said, "that Abigail will have a substantial dowry with which to marry. Would that not make a difference?"

Petrus shook his head. "I couldn't do that. It would be living off of her money. No, I cannot marry without a fortune of my own."

The young novice sat silently for a moment. Then he spoke, carefully and slowly. "I have a fortune of my own," he said.

"No, Nico, no, I couldn't," said Petrus. "It was your father's and now it is yours . . ."

"It is a great burden to me," said Nicolas, truthfully. "I cannot enter the church as a priest if I have wealth of my own, and becoming a priest is the highest honor I could aspire to."

"You? A priest? Congratulations, Nico!" exclaimed Petrus, momentarily brightening from the gloom which had now become his habit. "I knew you would make a good career in the church! I only wish I had done half as well as you."

"It is a calling, not a prize to be won," said Nicolas. "But, yes, I am going to be a priest. I have little further use for my worldly wealth. That is why I would like you to have it."

"Nico, you don't mean it! Are you sure? I mean, absolutely sure?"

"You would be doing me an immense favor by accepting it," said Nicolas. "After all, you need a great fortune to support your chariots, your horses, your fine clothes, and your elegant mansion."

Petrus laughed. "I have none of those things!"

"You have now," said Nicolas. "Let us go into town and

179

have the papers drawn up this very afternoon. Mind, you must swear to tell no one where it came from. And let me offer you this bit of advice — give as much to the poor and needy as you can. You will feel so much better."

The accountant, Ahmed, rolled his eyes and shook his head, indicating his complete disapproval of the arrangement, but in the end Nicolas had everything his way. The principal would go to Petrus on his twenty-fourth birthday, and young Maximus could borrow on the interest until that time. Nicolas requested that a portion only of the interest remain in his name.

"I thought you didn't need money," commented Petrus as they left the financial section of town. "What are you keeping it for?"

"There is unfinished business to take care of," said Nicolas, slyly. "The Lord's business."

CHAPTER SIXTEEN:

The Second Christmas Gift

The two seventeen-year-old young men stood before the monument to Senator Sergius Maximus. It stood nearly six feet high and ironically bore a Christian cross on the top. It was the largest, most noticeable, and most expensive monument that money could buy—a final tribute on the part of a living son to a deceased father.

"I hated him," said Petrus. "He was the cruelest type of human being you could imagine. He was greedy, selfish, arrogant—" The young man trailed off.

"Are you describing your father, or you?" asked Nicolas.

"Why must you always ask the hard questions?"

"Call it the duty of a friend."

"If I turned out the way I did, it was because of him. I'm glad he's dead. Good riddance."

"You have laid his ashes to rest. Now you must bury the hatred along with him. He cannot hurt you anymore."

"This is true," mused Petrus, thoughtfully.

"For my part, I feel sorry for him," said Nicolas.

"Sorry? For that monster?"

"It's true he was cruel. I will never forget the night he beat us. And he did not treat your mother properly. However, just imagine—in order to inflict that much pain, how much pain must *he* have had inside him? He would have to have been living in utter misery for years before he met your mother or sired you, in order to be that vindictive. Think of *his* hurt, of *his* pain."

"Nico, do you never think ill of *anyone?*"

Nicolas laughed. "I once asked that question of my father. Never did I think I would ever understand him. And now you are asking me the same question. I must be more like him than I thought."

"Well, I've discharged my last obligation to the old tyrant, anyhow. I've given him a decent burial in Christian ground — though he wasn't a Christian — and I've raised him a monument that will cause his name to be remembered long after you and I are gone. I don't need to do another thing for my father. I can get on with my own life now."

He and Nicolas started walking back toward the monastery. Petrus wore a fine black cloak with gold trim, an elegant black toga, and expensive black shoes. He once more looked like the young popinjay he had always tried to be. Since the restoration of his fortunes, much of the old arrogance and swagger had returned.

"*What* part of your life do you plan to get on with?" asked Nicolas, challengingly.

"I don't know what you mean," said Petrus, in a tone of feigned innocence.

"When do you plan to get married?" came the blunt question.

"I — I don't know," Petrus blurted out, abruptly. "When — when I'm ready."

"You were ready enough when you were a novice," said Nicolas. "You were ready enough to compromise your Christian values and turn your beloved into little more than a harlot!"

"Steady on," said Petrus. "I never compromised —"

"You compromised her virtue twice! Or was it three times? Or were there times I didn't know about?" went on Nicolas, heatedly. "She was a young girl who didn't know what she was doing, but you were supposed to be a man of God! You knew the rules, yet you broke them anyway! And ever since you left her honor in question, you have failed to do the right thing by her. You've left her dangling on hooks, living with empty promises. She gave herself to you, yet you will not make it right by honoring her."

"I didn't love her," confessed Petrus. "I do now. I was first in love with her sister."

"Ana?" gasped Nicolas, in disbelief.

"No, the elder. Angelina. She was my first true love. I wanted to marry her. Then she cast me aside, because of the contract her father had made with the family of that Slavic prince."

"Was that the reason you wanted to enter the monastery?" asked Nicolas.

"Partly. The other reason was—"

"—your father," finished Nicolas for him.

Petrus nodded. "He'd gotten too unbearable. He beat me nearly every day, and would allow me no freedom whatsoever. Without mother to soften things between us, life became—"

"—Hell," breathed Nicolas, softly.

"Yes," said Petrus. "So I figured that if you were having so much success as a novice in the monastery, I could, too. I did really want to be a good monk, you know."

"I'm sure you did," said Nicolas. "At least, part of you did."

"Then, on that Sunday after mass, when I saw that pompous prince looking lovingly at the girl I wanted, I—I got angry. I turned my attentions to the next girl available, who happened to be—"

"Abigail," finished Nicolas.

"Yes," said Petrus. "Ana was too young, you see. Not quite developed yet. And Abigail appeared to be so ripe for the—"

The young novice coughed twice, deliberately. "Let's skip that part, shall we?"

"Anyway, you saw us that afternoon. Nothing really happened, but I could tell she liked me, and that was all I wanted then—for her to like me. It didn't matter that I didn't like her. I just wanted to get back at Angelina and that Slav. From that point on, every opportunity I could find, I took. You know what happened at the inn, and later, in the chapel. Well, I—through all that I grew to respect her, though you may not believe it. By the time I proposed to her, I had come to love her."

"This doesn't explain why you won't marry her now," said Nicolas. "You have your fortune, and she is ready and willing."

It was Petrus' turn to cough in embarrassment. "Well, you see, now she's—she's poor."

"Eleven months ago you wouldn't marry her because *you* were too poor. Now you won't because *she* is too poor."

"She has no dowry," pointed out Petrus. "That windfall you hinted at hasn't come about. You don't expect me to marry a girl who brings nothing to the marriage, do you?"

"I suppose not," said Nicolas, with a sigh.

It was nearly Christmas. Another year had rolled around. In May, Sergius Maximus and his son had rejoiced in their newly restored wealth. Petrus had told his father, in one of the latter's more coherent moments, that the money had come from an investment that had prospered. (This was the truth—except that it had happened two generations earlier.) With the rise in prosperity and status, some degree of rationality had returned to the father and for a time an uneasy alliance had existed between the former Senator and his son while their life seemed to return to a semblance of what it had been before the great losses had been felt. Then in September, in a fit of anger against a servant, Sergius had misjudged his ability with a whip and had gotten it wrapped around his neck. With his air cut off, he was unable to breathe and thus fell to the floor in a faint. He had struck his head against the edge of a whipping-post and sunk into a coma, in which state he remained until the early part of December, when he breathed his last breath.

Having done his part to help lay the father to rest, Nicolas turned his thoughts to the son. There was no doubt that Petrus was a rascal! It seemed the black-haired boy would never really change. Yet Nicolas had to admit that his friend had a point. If the first daughter had married with a dowry, why not the second?

He had known all along what he would have to do. It had briefly been his hope that another Christmas Eve mission would not be necessary, thus freeing the money for other uses. However, it seemed inevitable that the Dorius girls should each have their dowries. And Petrus was no help.

Once again, the Head Novice asked the Abbot's permission to leave the monastery during midnight mass on Christmas Eve, claiming the Lord's business. And once again, the Abbot agreed, this time with a knowing wink.

Brother Marcus again had the horse ready. "This is getting to be a Christmas custom," joked the stable master.

Nicolas rode Cadeau through the streets of Patara, until he reached the familiar little house. However, some changes had been made in that little house over the previous year. Heavy curtains hung over the windows on the inside, keeping the light within from the view of passersby, while on the outside were newly-painted, tightly-fitting shutters. The house had likewise been painted and overall presented a much more pleasing appearance than it had the year before. Evidently Florus had decided that to move back to their former home would be to push his luck, and so he and his daughters had done their best to make improvements on the accommodations they already had.

There was no helpful crack in the window shutter, so Nicolas had to open it a little way from the outside to see what went on within. Ana and Abigail sat together by the fire, the wolfhound resting its head in Ana's lap while Abigail read aloud from a piece of paper. Their stockings had already been washed and hung up to dry.

"What else does she say?" asked Ana, eagerly, gently stroking the white fur of the dog's head.

"She has made a great success as a hostess in Novgorod society," said Abigail. "She and Korin are much loved by their people. There is talk that Korin's father will appoint him to an important political position in the New Year."

"That means they won't be able to visit us," said Ana, a little sadly.

"Yes, they will!" exclaimed Abigail, reading further. "They are coming for a visit in the spring! Prince Ilyan is coming, too." The middle sister cast a sly look at the younger. Ana blushed.

Outside, Nicolas felt suddenly stung as if by a pin prick.

"And—oh, this is wonderful!" cried Abigail. "A baby is expected soon. That is why they cannot travel until the spring. She will bring the child when she comes, so that we can see it, and so that it can see its grandfather. Oh, won't Papa be proud!"

Then a silence fell between them, as Abigail put down the letter.

"It sounds as if Angelina is having all of the fun," observed Ana.

Abigail sighed.

"Cheer up. He will ask for you again. They say he has tons of money, much more than he ever had before."

"But he will not marry a girl with no dowry," complained Abigail. "I am in the same position Angelina was in a year ago."

"An angel helped us out before. An angel will do so again," declared Ana, firmly.

"How do you know?" asked Abigail.

"Because I will pray again, and then the money will come, just as it did last Christmas."

"Miracles never happen twice," scoffed Abigail. "Besides, I—I'm not sure I deserve a miracle. I—I haven't been the good girl that Angelina was. God can hardly be expected to have good things in store for *me*."

"God has good things for all of us," said Ana, stoutly. "Angelina is not perfect, either. Think of what she was planning to do to support us before the miracle happened. Yet God had other plans for her. He knows we are weak creatures and we need help, and that is why I am confident He will help us again."

Moments later, the second sister retired to her chamber. The youngest, as before, went to the window. Young Ana had grown noticeably over the past year, and at thirteen had begun to blossom into a young woman. Nicolas felt a little tug at his heart as he crouched beneath the window and listened to the prayer of the girl he loved.

"Blessed Jesus," prayed Ana, "send your angel to help us once more. Last year I prayed for my elder sister and for our family, and you answered my prayer. Now I pray for a dowry for my second sister. Oh, dear Lord, I know you will answer me as you did before!"

When Ana had retired for the night, Nicolas again set to work. He had a little more difficulty prying the new shutter open, but finally he succeeded, and crept inside.

"R-r-r-r-r-r-r-r."

The wolfhound stood growling, as if daring him to take one more step, just as the dog had done the previous year. This time, from the folds of his robe, Nicolas produced a big, juicy bone he had procured in the marketplace. The dog at once snatched the treat from the intruder's hand and began gnawing away at it in a corner of the room. Nicolas slipped the bag of gold into a stocking he guessed belonged to Abigail. This time, instead of thirty gold pieces, there were only twenty-nine and some change, as one coin had been used to purchase the bone.

As before, when his task was done, he slipped out of the house through the window and closed the shutters. Riding off through the streets, he wondered how many more Christmas Eves he would have to spend delivering gifts.

CHAPTER SEVENTEEN:

The Boy Priest

Nicolas' years in the monastery reached their ultimate fulfillment in February, two months after his seventeenth birthday. His ordination ceremony took place with great pomp and circumstance, and as the ceremonial robes were placed about his shoulders he felt as though he had reached the pinnacle of his career. No more would he be a lowly novice, stable hand, or kitchen apprentice. From now on he would be addressed as "Father" and he would be in charge of others, no longer as a mere Head Novice, but as a spiritual leader. He did not feel proud, but rather justified, as though his vocation had at long last been confirmed. He had become a priest of the Holy Church.

In attendance, besides Abbot Stephanus, who ordained him, and the other monks and novices, he observed his best friend and closest companion Petrus Maximus, and the remaining daughters of Florus' household, accompanied by their father. Petrus stood close to Abigail, his hand clasped around hers. At the very back stood an elderly couple, whose faces seemed friendly and familiar, but whom Nicolas could not for the moment place. Some friends of his late parents, he assumed. Scores of other well-wishers from the parish had come as well, and Nicolas felt gratified to see such a turnout for his special day.

Heart and soul remained in conflict. As he glanced from one to the other of the congregation, his eye most often rested on the fresh and lovely face of Ana, at thirteen a child no more.

The beloved of his heart had eyes only for him, it seemed, in the way she gazed at the golden-haired young man in rapt admiration. She looked at him as though he possessed the very spirit of Christ and all His angels. It reminded Nicolas of the story his mother and father had often told, how as a newborn infant he had reached out his arms toward Heaven while a great light had radiated all around him. Ana appeared to be seeing a similar vision. Perhaps the sunlight streaming through the window had caught his hair, enhancing with its beams the natural color, and creating the effect of a halo. Such had happened before, on less auspicious occasions, and the brothers had teased him about being an angel in their midst. He could think of no other way to account for Ana's apparent fascination.

He loved her, even if he would only admit the fact to himself. Guilt feelings plagued him constantly about his decision. Was he to reach the apex of his spiritual career, only to disgrace himself even more disastrously than his friend had done a little more than a year and a half earlier? Would he later choose to abandon his post in order to enjoy the pleasures of the flesh with the girl of his dreams? Now he understood fully the reason for Abbot Stephanus' insistence that he meet as many young women of his age as possible before taking his final vows.

He wanted to go to her and tell her of his feelings. He longed to caress her, put his arms around her, and kiss her sweet lips. He longed to satisfy the sexual drive within that pushed him to consider compromising his vocation to pursue the greatest love of his life.

But no—*she* was not the greatest love of his life. His love for Christ, the Holy One, outweighed any human love he could ever know. Ever since that encounter in the darkness when he was but a child and throughout his years of growing up, the Light of the World had been his master and his guide. The roots of his faith grew in deep soil. He loved Ana, yes, but he loved the Lord more.

Gazing at her as she gazed up at him, he knew he would

have to let her go. He could never tell her of his love, nor could he ever seek to win her heart. In God's good order, it was not ordained that he should take a wife. What was ordained was represented by the robes of ceremony which he now wore, and by the words which Abbot Stephanus spoke over him, and by the public declaration of his vows, confirmed now and forever. He was God's property now. He belonged to the world no longer.

"Well done, Father Nicolas," said Petrus, as he privately congratulated his friend after the ceremony. "At least one of us has fulfilled the dream of taking final vows."

"You will be taking some vows soon yourself, if what I hear is true," said Nicolas.

Petrus nodded. "It is. I am going to marry Abigail."

"So at last, old friend, all our dreams are coming to pass."

"I hope so," said Petrus.

Nicolas had assumed that he would take a secondary part in Petrus' wedding. Abbot Stephanus had presided over weddings in the parish for many, many years, and had performed the ceremony for the eldest daughter of Florus. The young priest had imagined that he would read from the scriptures or light a couple of candles. It surprised and gratified him when the Abbot informed him that, as a priest, he, Nicolas, had the authority to perform marriages and further, that he was expected to perform this one. Stephanus then told his nephew to start preparing for the event, learning the proper prayers and memorizing the words of the marriage ceremony. The young priest thanked his mentor profusely for the opportunity. To think that his first wedding would be that of his lifelong best friend! Nicolas could not have imagined any greater assignment.

A late spring date was set, so that Angelina, her husband, and his family could attend. To this Petrus readily agreed. In fact, he found himself agreeing to a great many things in preparation for the memorable day, most notably expenditures. When a need arose, Abigail would not hesitate either to ask her husband-to-be to take care of it, or to give her the money so that she could take care of it. She wanted certain flowers, certain material for the gowns, certain dainties to be served to the guests—every item of which cost a small fortune in and of itself. Having received one good thing, in the form of her dowry, Abigail had begun to feel deserving of more, and more, and more. Her demands often grew into the form of nagging, but Petrus would sigh, agree to go along with her wishes, and hand over the money. He wished the whole thing would hurry up and be over.

At last the great day drew near. "Tomorrow at this time," he announced to Nicolas, "I will be a married man." The two friends sat in a study not unlike the one occupied by Father Stephanus. The seventeen-year-old priest shared a glass of wine with the seventeen-year-old bridegroom. Petrus sighed as he sipped his wine. "I hope it proves to be worth all of the bother."

"Bother? There is nothing wrong, I hope," said Nicolas.

"Nothing, except piles and piles of bills from merchants and shopkeepers. Abigail spends money even faster than I do."

"It is immaterial," said Nicolas. "You have plenty to spare—as I well know."

"I won't for long, at the rate she's going. I'm tired of her spending, Nico. I'm tired of being the center of everyone's attention—or rather, of my *bride's* being the center of everyone's attention. Most of all, I'm tired of hearing about that wretched miracle."

"Miracle?" asked Nicolas.

"Yes," said Petrus. "Surely you've heard the story. It's the talk of all Patara. The story of how first the eldest daughter found a sackful of coins for her dowry in her stocking when she awoke on Christmas morning. It seems the second daughter like-wise found a dowry in the same manner the following year."

"It's indeed a miracle," marveled Nicolas. "God is surely generous and good."

"People say that a good angel blesses the Dorius family," said Petrus. "The problem is that the tale's popularity, through endless repetitions, has gone to Abigail's head. Every time she retells it, she embellishes it a little more. At first, it was the work of an unknown benefactor. Now to hear it, she talks as if the money had been delivered by the Angel Gabriel! I'm sure before long she will be spreading rumors that the Christ Child Himself brings gifts at Christmas."

"She has a grateful heart," mused Nicolas. "It's only natural for her to want to tell of her good fortune."

"Come off it, Nico! It was you, wasn't it?"

"What do you mean?"

"You had the money. You wanted us to get married. It bothered you that I did not want to marry a dowerless girl. You felt that I had compromised her honor. So you paid a midnight visit to the Dorius house and hid the money. Am I right?"

"I won't lie," said Nicolas.

"Then it *was* you! I thought so!"

Nicolas put a finger to his lips. "Tell no one . . . not even your bride. Let people go on thinking of it as a miracle."

"You did it for me, didn't you? Just as you gave me all of your—well, most of your money."

The young priest nodded. "Partly for you. And partly for her."

"I don't know whether to bless or curse you," laughed Petrus. "When she came running to me on Christmas day to tell me of her good fortune, I swept her up into my arms then and there, I kissed her, and I proposed to marry her. Now I am well and truly stuck, and I must make good my part of the bargain."

"Not for one minute do I think you are stuck. I believe the two of you will be very happy together, as happy as my parents were."

"And as happy as you are in your newly-attained priesthood?" asked Petrus, with a sly look.

"Why do you look at me like that? I am very happy and contented following God's calling." Nicolas shifted uneasily in his chair.

"Yes, my friend," said Petrus. "As am I, in taking a wife." He gave another sly look, as though implying more than his words said.

The day of the wedding dawned with a brilliant sky. Balmy breezes lightly stirred the trees and brought a mild respite from the warmth of the spring sunshine. The wedding guests arrived. Such an assemblage of finery had seldom been seen at the chapel. Chariots drawn by teams of two, four, and even six horses pulled up to the gate. Women emerged clad in elegant gowns, men in handsome togas, noble folk attended by humbly yet neatly-dressed servants and slaves. Abbot Stephanus, having little to do, greeted the guests effusively as they arrived, and the holy brothers in their simple black robes escorted the guests to their seats.

The Maximus chariot arrived and the bridegroom stepped out. Petrus wore a black toga with gold trim and a magnificent white cloak. He had none of the smirking look of the mischievous boy about him as he strode with dignity toward the chapel.

The Dorius family then arrived, accompanied by the visiting members of the Koratovich family. Guests lingering outside the chapel crowded to see Angelina's new infant son, who had been christened with the name Dmitri. Prince Korin walked stiffly and proudly by the side of his wife and offspring. Florus escorted the bride, who radiated beauty in a long, silvery gown made of exquisite silks imported from the East. Prince Ilyan, the reddish tones of his hair highlighted by the bright sun, gallantly walked arm-in-arm with Ana, the simplicity of whose gown could not diminish her natural charm and grace. The two exchanged many fond smiles.

All was in readiness. The altar had been prepared, and re-prepared, until it lived up to Father Nicolas' demanding specifications. The brothers who played the music on flute and lyre had been made to practice their pieces over and over. The young priest himself had spent hours memorizing the words of the service, until he could recite them flawlessly without reference to the books or scrolls.

As he gazed about the full chapel, Nicolas' confidence began to flag. "I am afraid, Father Stephanus," he whispered to his mentor. "What if I make a mistake? What if I do something wrong?"

"I am here at your elbow should you need me," said Stephanus, reassuringly. "Of course you won't, because you are my nephew and you possess greater gifts than mine. God be with you, my son."

"Thank you, Reverend Father," whispered Nicolas.

The ceremony was ready to begin. The bride stood at the altar, accompanied by her father, who was giving her away. The bridesmaids, including the bride's sister Ana, stood in attendance just behind. The groom's supporters, among whom numbered Prince Korin and Prince Ilyan, the future brothers-in-law, flanked the groom's side of the platform.

There remained only one person missing.

Murmurings began to arise from the crowd. The bride's look of anticipation had turned to one of anxiety. The groomsmen looked about them, as though expecting to discover the absentee in their midst.

Abbot Stephanus leaned over to Nicolas. "Where is young Maximus?" he whispered.

"I don't know," whispered Nicolas. "He was here a few minutes ago."

Just then Brother John tugged at the Abbot's sleeve, and informed him that two bottles of wine had disappeared from the cellar. One of the novices, hearing a noise below, had discovered that the wine cellar had been ransacked and had immediately reported the matter.

"What shall we do?" asked Brother John.

Abbot Stephanus shrugged. "Ask Father Nicolas," he said. "He is in charge today."

Brother John turned humbly to his former kitchen apprentice. Nicolas found it amusing that since the change in his status, the grumbling monk had become entirely deferential toward the new priest. "Father," he asked, humbly, "what is to be done in this matter?"

"I think I can solve two problems at once," said Nicolas. "I know where to find the bridegroom, and the two wine bottles." He quickly left the chapel and headed for the stairs that led to the novices' quarters.

He found Petrus, his cloak removed, seated on the stool next to the humble straw mat that had once been his own bed as he drank from one of the bottles. The other bottle lay empty on the floor.

"Petrus—"

"Go away," muttered the bridegroom.

"You can't do this, Petrus. Pull yourself together. People are waiting. Your bride is waiting."

"I don' wanna marry her," grumbled Petrus. "I'd rather go back to bein' a monk. I don' love her."

"You told me you did," said Nicolas.

"Well, I don.' I love Angelina, and I can' have her."

"No, you can't. She's a married woman, for Heaven's sake, with a child. Abigail is the one you are pledged to marry."

"Jus' leave me be," said Petrus. "I'm no good, I tell you. I won' be a fai'ful husband. I'll chea' on her, just like my father chea'ed on my mother."

"You'll do no such thing!" scolded Nicolas. "You're not like your father."

"Yes, I am," groaned Petrus. "I'm jus' like him. I'm cruel an' vindictive. I'm a wastrel an' a drunk!"

"No, you're not!" cried Nicolas, seizing the bottle forcibly and removing it from his friend's hand. Petrus struggled to hold onto it, but in his present state his reflexes were not quick enough. Nicolas set the bottle down, out of his friend's reach. "You're nothing like your father. You're kind, compassionate, a devoted friend, and an excellent companion. You're a very *good* man, Petrus. Not like him at all!"

"How?" asked Petrus, challengingly. "Wha's different about me?"

"You are a Christian," said Nicolas quietly.

Petrus appeared stunned, as though an invisible hand had struck an unexpected blow. "I—I am," he murmured, looking astonished at the truth of the thought. "I'm a Chris'ian, and I love God."

"Of course you do. You've been trying so hard to serve Him, and now He has given you an opportunity in which you can—as a married man, and a faithful, devoted husband, and (God willing) as a father. A kind, loving, good father."

"You're a father," said Petrus, thoughtfully.

"I'm your spiritual father now," said Nicolas. "And I hope to prove as good a one in my capacity as I know you will be in yours."

"Bless you, Father Nicolas," said Petrus, with a sudden grin. The young bridegroom sighed with relief.

"I give you five minutes to pull yourself together. If you're not in the chapel by then I'll—"

"You'll what?" asked Petrus, apparently more out of curiosity than a need to challenge.

"I'll excommunicate you!" threatened Nicolas, sternly. He didn't know if he had the power to excommunicate or not. He rather doubted it, but it made for a fine threat. Whether he would or could ever have carried it out was another matter. It accomplished its purpose. The thought of being unable to attend church, take part in Communion, or get into Heaven should he die an excommunicate, caused Petrus to turn pale. All at once their position had shifted from that of boyhood friends to that of priest and parishioner.

"Y—yes, Father," stammered the black-haired youth, cowed into instant obedience.

Nicolas returned to the chapel.

He scarcely recognized the bridegroom when Petrus finally made his appearance. The young man who had been scarcely able to stand up just minutes before now walked with dignity and an air of nobility. The face that had been hot, flushed, and stained with tears now shone with a rosy, fresh complexion. The cloak that had lain on the floor, crumpled and askew, now draped elegantly across a pair of erect shoulders. Petrus took his place by the side of his bride with a noble, even regal, bearing. As he gave a loving look to the young woman who would be his wife, his eyes looked clear and bright. Nicolas' original assessment of the boy he had glimpsed in the marketplace those many years ago now seemed to ring true. Here stood a prince—a true prince among men.

Speaking the words that knit Petrus and Abigail together as husband and wife, Father Nicolas kept his mind and his attention on the ceremony, ignoring to the best of his ability the fact that Ana's eyes were once again fixed upon him in a look of adoration. He strove to do his best, to remember every word in its place and to recite it correctly, and the effort kept his mind from dwelling on thoughts that were better left alone, especially at this special and sacred time.

Looking up from the prayer, Nicolas beheld, standing in the back of the chapel, the same elderly couple that had attended his ordination. They looked upon him with loving and adoring eyes. At once he realized who they were. No wonder they had seemed so familiar. They had come to bless him in his new ministry. They were his parents.

When next he looked in their direction, the two had vanished.

CHAPTER EIGHTEEN:

The Third Christmas Gift

"You gave us quite a fright at the wedding, young man," scolded Father Stephanus. "We thought you had changed your mind."

"I did," said Petrus, "but I changed it back. Thanks to some help from a friend." He beamed gratefully at Nicolas. "Sorry for being such a crybaby that day. I guess I'll never really outgrow my childishness, will I?"

"You have grown up in more ways than you will ever know," said Father Nicolas, "especially since being married. I told you that you would make a fine husband for Abigail. These last months you have become a man of character and responsibility. You have proven yourself a true prince, in spite of everything."

"Well, I didn't want to risk being excommunicated."

"Excommunicated?" Abbot Stephanus raised a quizzical eyebrow at his nephew.

"Just a little matter between Maximus and myself," said Nicolas, hastily.

"Will we ever meet again, do you suppose?" asked Petrus of his closest friend.

"God willing, we shall," said Nicolas.

The moment of parting had become awkward. Seven months had passed since the wedding, and now Petrus stood ready to take his leave of his best friend. The new husband

199

planned to take his new wife to Rome for a prolonged honeymoon. They did not know when they would return, for they both desired to stay in the ancient heart of the Empire for a while. Petrus had stopped by for a quick farewell that grew longer and more painful with each passing moment. When the realization actually hit both of them at once that their parting was at hand, everything became more difficult to say. What words could lifelong companions speak to one another that would suffice to commemorate the deep-rooted bond they shared?

"I—I'll feel a little lost without you, Nico," said Petrus, with a sudden catch in his voice. "I wouldn't be the man I am now if you hadn't helped me to find my way."

"And I would not alter one moment of our past together," said Nicolas. "Through you, and sometimes in spite of you, God has taught me much." He laughed a little, to hide the choke in his own throat, and hastily brushed away a tear that had formed in his eye.

All at once their many shared experiences rushed upon their mutual recollection, and they felt as though they could never be as whole apart as they had been together. Petrus threw himself into Nicolas' embrace, Nicolas clasped his companion in his arms, and the two friends hugged and blubbered like a pair of children. They held onto one another tightly, neither wanting to be the first to let go.

"Petrus!" shrieked a shrill voice from the chariot. "Will you come along now? I want to get to my sister's! She is waiting for us!"

Petrus heaved a sigh and broke loose. "Yes, my dearest," he called back, in as sweet a tone as he could muster. He shook his friend's hand firmly. "Farewell, Nico . . . Father Nicolas, I mean. And goodbye, Abbot Stephanus."

"Farewell, Petrus Maximus," said Nicolas. "May God's blessings ever go with you!"

Stephanus put a loving arm around his nephew's shoulder as they watched the chariot until it turned a corner and was gone from view. "There goes living proof of God's love at work," observed the Abbot. "That young man has undergone a mighty transformation in a short time."

"Do you think now he'll be able to stay out of trouble?" asked Nicolas.

"I don't think so," said the Abbot, good-naturedly. "If he didn't get into trouble now and then, he wouldn't be Petrus. But God will watch over him."

Just then, a novice appeared with the information that a visitor had arrived, and had requested an audience with the young priest.

Nicolas sighed. No doubt some parishioner wanted to make confession. Already since becoming a priest, he must have heard a thousand confessions. Still, it was part of his duty and he could not refuse. He looked at Father Stephanus, who dismissed him with a nod, and both went about their separate duties.

To his surprise, the visitor turned out to be Prince Ilyan Koratovich. The Prince had remained in Patara after his brother had taken the rest of the family back to the northern country.

"Good Father Nicolas," said the Prince, "I have come to you for guidance and counsel."

Nicolas ushered the young man into his study, and offered the newcomer a seat and a glass of wine.

Prince Ilyan accepted on both counts. When the Prince had gotten comfortable, Nicolas inquired as to the reason for the visit.

"I have asked to speak with you, Father Nicolas, because I know you are good and kind. You are close to God, yes?"

"I suppose you could say so," said Nicolas, uneasy about what the visitor could be leading up to.

"I come to you because I don't know who else to turn to. I am miserable."

"What is the matter?" asked Nicolas, politely.

"If you remember, I told you before that I was in love, no? And we prayed for a miracle, here in the monastery. Do you remember how excited I was on that Christmas when our prayer was answered? The dowry that came from Heaven was enough to allow Angelina to marry. The next year, the same miracle happened for Abigail."

"What is your concern now?"

"I am afraid that a third miracle might prove too much to ask," said Ilyan. "You see, as I told you, I wish to marry Ana."

Nicolas' heart groaned, but he made no outward indication of it.

"My family will not permit me to marry her unless she has a dowry of her own. This is something her father cannot give her. Angelina and Abigail have both offered to contribute out of what is left of their own dowries, but it will not be enough. I wanted to loan Ana the money, but my family forbids it."

"The girl is young yet," said Nicolas. "Her sisters were older when they married. I believe she cannot be fourteen yet. There is no hurry."

"She is fourteen," said Ilyan, "and my heart tells me there is reason to hurry. I am in love, you see, and she is in love with me. She is grown now, nearly a woman, and it is not too early. I am fifteen—nearly sixteen—and a grown man. Christmas is approaching, and I greatly desire to be engaged in the New Year so that we may be married in the spring."

"I still see no urgency," said Nicolas. "You both have years ahead of you."

"Forgive me, Father, but you are so holy and good you do not know what it is like to be in love."

Oh, don't I? thought Nicolas, ruefully. Hesitantly, he asked aloud, "Are—are you certain that this is what she wants? To marry you?"

"Yes," said the prince, earnestly. "She has agreed to become my wife, if ever she can. She says that in all the world there is but one person she could love more—and that is the mysterious benefactor who has blessed her two sisters."

Nicolas led the prince in a perfunctory prayer, requesting that God's will be done in the matter. Prince Ilyan went on his way, feeling hopeful—for the young priest's prayers had a history of success—but leaving Nicolas with a sad and bitter heart.

He stubbornly fought against the idea of making yet another Christmas Eve visit to the Dorius house. Yet what other choice did he have? He had long since committed himself to taking care of this family. It would be rather cruel, he realized, to leave the third daughter penniless, after he had already blessed the elder two.

But in so doing, he would forever squelch the possibility of finding a soul mate in the person of the beautiful Ana. He would be setting her on a path of life that would permanently take her away from him and his world.

She did not love him. How could she, a lay person, possibly be in love with a priest? The notion may never have crossed her mind, or her heart. Yet there had been those times when she had stared at him as though his were the face of Christ and he alone were the key to her salvation. Surely she loved, in a deep, devout way. And such a love might mean that a greater passion lay beneath. It might even mean that he was the one great love of her life.

Was it wrong for him, as a priest, to oppose the girl's marriage? He wanted, as he told himself, only what was best for her. And for her to marry, while yet a child, and bind herself to this pompous, arrogant, wealthy young Slav . . . but no, he realized. Prince Ilyan may have dressed in fine clothes, and borne himself with a manly, noble demeanor, but he was not arrogant, nor was he pompous. The boy had a generosity of spirit that Nicolas felt put himself to shame. Had Ilyan not played host to two young disgraced novices, after having been immersed in filth by them both, and assisted them to recover themselves after their months of punishment? Such forgiveness showed nobility that proved Ilyan to have a maturity beyond his years. No, he was not pompous, nor arrogant, nor anything undesirable. In fact, if

Ana were to look for years and years, she would be unlikely to find a young man with a more charitable, loving, Christian heart. Could the young Slav, after all, be God's choice for the girl?

And was not God's will more important than the will of Nicolas? Every good thing, as he had learned so long ago, had a price. Was not this the price of priesthood—to make sacrifices beyond those expected of ordinary mortals? If it was God's best plan for Ana and for Ilyan, did Nicolas have any right to oppose it, or stand in its way? And besides, she didn't have to marry the prince or anyone else once she had the money. It would be hers to do with as she chose. And should not that choice be given to her, and then left up to her? If God's hand were in the matter, as Nicolas knew it was, then he himself would be, as before, but the humble instrument of God's generosity. As a priest, it should have been his joyous obligation to carry out the will of God. *Go thou, and take my gifts to the world . . .*

Nicolas went to the Abbot. "Reverend Father," he began.

Abbot Stephanus' face broke into a broad smile. "Let me guess," he said. "You wish to be excused from the midnight mass on Christmas Eve, because you have the Lord's business to do."

Nicolas nodded.

The Abbot carefully scrutinized his nephew's face. "Have you anything else to tell me?" he asked, probingly. The young priest wondered if the older man knew anything of his forbidden love. He must have suspected, or he wouldn't have asked the question. Here was the chance for Nicolas to relieve himself of the burden of his secret guilt. He nearly blurted it all out. The words played upon his lips for a fleeting moment, but fear of the possible consequences held his tongue in check.

Nicolas averted his eyes. "No, Father," he said meekly. This was one problem he would have to work out on his own.

"Very well," said Stephanus. The Abbot's tone suggested that he knew Nicolas struggled with some issue or other, but that he would let the young priest keep his own counsel and would not pry uninvited into a matter that the boy chose not to discuss. Then he added, with a hearty laugh, "Your mission is for the best, for this one's the prettiest of the lot. But tell me, my son, what will you do with yourself *next* Christmas Eve?"

The young priest smiled one of his rare smiles. "Probably attend the midnight mass!" he replied, blithely.

He emerged from the monastery into a still, warm night on the eve of the celebration of Christ's birth. He padded across the courtyard in his bare feet, the gold strapped inside his robe jingling as he walked. Once again, Brother Marcus had the white horse saddled and ready. "Your yearly midnight rides have become a tradition," remarked the holy brother as he helped the young priest with the boots and the cloak. "I think instead of Father Nicolas, they should call you Father Christmas!"

"This is the last time," promised Nicolas.

Brother Marcus shook his head. "Once a giftbringer, always a giftbringer," he said. "I do not think you will find it so easy to stop what you have started."

Nicolas mounted Cadeau and bade good evening to Brother Marcus. Then he rode out of the monastery courtyard and into the streets of the city. The horse, who seemed always to know the way to the Dorius house, kept up a steady pace while the rider maintained a relaxed hold on the reins. They passed many parishioners who were on their way to midnight mass. This time, however, the people did not mostly mill past him without a second look. As a novice, he had enjoyed a degree of anonymity—he had been just one holy brother taking a brisk Christmas Eve canter. Now, however, he realized that he had gained considerable notoriety. Many recognized the eighteen-year-old priest from the monastery. He heard occasional murmurings and whisperings as he rode past groups of hurrying churchgoers. His ears picked up snatches of their conversations about him.

"There goes the boy priest on his white horse."

"Where do you suppose he could be going on Christmas Eve?"

"Probably to visit the sick, or to help a friend."

"His good works are well known in Patara."

"He is young, but he is kind and charitable."

"What is his name?"

"Father Nicolas."

He realized, as he overheard these comments, that a new complication had arisen this year. People would remember having seen him riding through the streets. Any "miracles" that took place this night would be certain, sooner or later, to be attributed to him. Well, it was too late to adopt a disguise or to find less crowded streets to ride through. He would have to brave it out, and let people say or think what they would.

Reaching the quiet street where the modest house of Florus stood, Nicolas noticed that considerably more changes had taken place in the past year. More repair and refurbishing had been done to it. The house now looked truly comfortable. Clearly the brides had not used all of their dowry money for wedding expenses.

Tethering the horse, he noticed that another steed had been tied close by. He wondered if Florus or his daughter had visitors. He crept up to the window and tried to peer inside. No light shone from within through the heavy curtains, and the shutters held no cracks big enough to see through, so he could not tell whether or not the family had gone to bed. When he gently tried to pry a shutter open, he found it tightly locked. The same proved true of the second shutter. He went around the outside of the house, trying window after window, but found them all shut and securely locked. Just as he had tried the last one, he heard the sound of the front door opening. He sank back into the shadows.

Prince Ilyan stepped out of the house. He kissed Ana, who remained just within, and letting go of her hand, bade her a loving good night. The wolfhound stood at the girl's feet, sniffing the night air. "All will yet be well between us, my love," declared Ilyan. I believe in your good angel."

"So do I," replied Ana, uneasily. "But dare we hope for a third miracle?"

"The good Father Nicolas has prayed a prayer for us," stated Ilyan, with conviction. "It was his prayer that brought about the first miracle, so I have great confidence in his ability to pray."

"*His* prayer?" gasped Ana. "I thought our benefactor had come in response to *my* prayer."

"Your prayers helped, I am sure," said Ilyan. "But Father Nicolas' powerful prayers have been with us all along. He has prayed and prayed for your family's continued blessing and well-being."

A glow of ecstasy lit up Ana's face. "Oh, God bless him! God bless the good Father Nicolas! He is a saint, to devote so much time in prayer on our behalf. He is a good man, and a kind man, and I love him dearly!"

Nicolas' heart raced as he heard these words. He tried, with little success, not to read too much into them. After all, she had just let Ilyan kiss her. But to know that he occupied some place in her heart was almost too much for him to bear. He couldn't help wishing and hoping that she truly loved him in a permanent way as much as she had now declared in a momentary burst of affection.

"I wish you could speak with such warmth of your love for me," said Ilyan, a trace of reproach in his voice.

"I—I love you, Ilyan," said Ana. "I—I do, truly. And I promise to make you a good wife."

"That is all any man can ask of the woman he loves." Kissing her hand, then walking away backwards for several paces, Ilyan waved farewell to his beloved, then mounted his horse and rode off. The white stallion had been tied at a little distance, so if the prince thought anything of the sight of another steed, he probably assumed that one of the neighbors had a visitor on this holiday night.

As she went inside, Ana neglected to shut the door firmly, so that conversation between the girl and her father drifted out to where Nicolas could hear.

"Yes, Father," said Ana, firmly. "I do want to marry him. He loves me so much."

"But do you love him?" asked Florus, gently.

"I think so," said the girl. "I believe I do."

"You hesitate. Is there someone you love more?"

"No, not really . . . except, well, yes, there is one person I love more, and that is our good angel."

"Ana, you cannot fall in love with an angel. An angel is not flesh and blood."

"Do you think it is an angel, then? A real angel, from Heaven?"

"I have no way of knowing, one way or another," admitted Florus. "I suspect that he is as mortal as you or I. However, God works in mysterious ways."

"But if he were a real person, a real man, I would love him," said Ana. "I would love him more than life itself."

Does she really mean what she says? wondered Nicolas. *Should I proceed with my plan, or am I throwing away all of my chances for happiness?* If he felt certain her heart was his, he might have abandoned his mission then and there, rushed forward, revealed himself, and claimed her as his own. However, he felt bound by his original decision to help all three girls in their time of need without their knowledge of his intervention. As a man of God, he had to follow what was right. As a man of flesh, he had desires that would not be satisfied with anything less than complete gratification. The conflict within momentarily froze him into indecision, until another expediency forced him into action.

The wolfhound nosed its way out the door, opening it

far enough to get through. The dog sniffed the night air suspiciously, and began to bark.

Nicolas grabbed the bone he had tucked away in his robes and used it to lure the animal to him. The hound recognized the scent of its benefactor of the previous year, so it stopped barking, and did not growl or bite, but trotted up to Nicolas and licked his hand before accepting the bone. Then the creature settled down to gnaw earnestly at the juiciest treat it had known since last Christmas.

"It's past midnight, Ana," said Florus. "We should be in bed."

"Where is Boris?" asked Ana. "I don't see him anywhere."

"He may have gone out. You left the door open."

Ana stepped outside of the house. Nicolas pressed back into the shadows. "Boris!" she called. "Boris!"

The dog, hearing its name, barked once, as if to say "Don't bother me!" and continued to gnaw on the bone.

"Oh, there you are!" exclaimed Ana, coming forward toward her pet.

Breathing as inaudibly as he could, Nicolas resisted the impulse to burst out of hiding, fold her in his arms, and proclaim his love for her. Now that she stood so near to him, he desperately wanted—with *nearly* all his heart—to do just that. His heart pounded fiercely, as though it were trying to burst through his rib cage. His breathing grew heavier, as if he had just run a dozen miles. Sweat poured down his brow. He did not move, although it required every ounce of willpower to keep himself in check.

Ana continued to address her pet. "Come inside at once, you naughty dog!"

Reluctantly, the dog got up, carrying its bone in its teeth, and followed its mistress inside the house.

"Look, Papa. Boris has found a bone. I wonder where he could have gotten it."

"It must have fallen off a meat merchant's wagon."

"You know very well no merchants come down this street."

"Then perhaps it is a gift from the good Christmas angel," said Florus, with a gentle laugh. "At any rate, it is high time for my youngest daughter to be in her bed. Have you washed and hung up your stockings, like a good girl?"

"Yes, Papa," said Ana. Her tone of voice indicated that she didn't at all mind being slightly patronized in this way, even though far from being a child.

"Be off, then," said the father, and she must have obeyed him, for Nicolas heard no further conversation. A moment later, Florus himself appeared in the doorway, as he pulled the door tight, and once it had been shut, Nicolas heard a bolt sliding into place.

He waited nearly an hour, to make sure that the father and daughter had fallen asleep. In that time, he devised a bold plan for getting the sack of gold into the house. Since the windows and door were locked, he would have to try the roof. He untied Cadeau and brought the animal close to the house. Then he managed to stand up on the horse's back. The horse stood very still, as though understanding the situation perfectly. Nicolas could just reach the edge of the roof in this manner. Fortunately, the house had a flat roof so that he could scramble onto it with all of the agility of his eighteen years. Once on top, he scanned the roof for possible points of entry, but found none. The only opening came from the chimney over the fireplace, where wisps of smoke continued to float upward from the dying embers.

He had feared that this would prove to be the only point where entry would be possible, but he was determined to deliver his gift one way or another, and without being known. Stealthily, he made his way across the rooftop and peered down the chimney. It was large and wide, fashioned in rectangular Roman shape and made of sun-dried brick. The chimney afforded ample room for his slender body. The bricks offered sturdy handholds and footholds. The smoke had thinned enough so that it would not choke him. And the blackness of his robes would not be noticeably disfigured by the soot.

He put a tentative leg over the rim and tested his first foothold. The bricks proved able to bear his weight. So he climbed over the top of the chimney and lowered himself inside, standing with one foot on one foothold while he felt with his other foot for another. His left leg pained him as it had often done since the day of the chariot accident, and favoring it made his movements awkward as he gingerly took each downward step. He was glad nobody could observe him. He took one step down, then another, then another, steadying himself by holding onto bricks with his hands as he felt for fresh steps with his feet. His face brushed against the sides of the chimney until he felt grimy with soot. Down, down, down he went. The smoke grew thicker the nearer he got to the fireplace, and he tried not to breathe it, but he could not avoid inhaling some of it. The air in the chimney grew stifling.

Finally, he neared the bottom. His difficulty breathing made it harder and harder for him to concentrate on securing a foothold. Suddenly, a brick came away in his hand. He lost his footing and tumbled downward, landing on top of the hot coals. He tried to muffle his cries of pain by stuffing portions of his robe into his mouth, but after doing so he quickly turned his attention to scattering the coals, and shaking out the ones that had gotten caught in the robe. The next moment he had to contend with a small flame that quickly grew into a big one, burning a great hole in his garment. Endeavoring to make as little noise as possible, he twisted the robe until it hung slightly off of him and then beat the flame out against the wall of the chimney. As the pain of the short, sharp contact with the coals subsided, he spit out the portion of robe from his mouth, and tried to adjust his clothing until it draped properly, discovering to his dismay that the hole had burnt through in an embarrassing place. Ankle-deep in ashes, and covered from head to toe with grime and soot, with a hole in the rear end of his robe, he felt like a complete fool.

Hearing someone stirring in a nearby room, he quickly went about his task. Not having time to stuff the bag of money in a stocking, he tucked it into one of Ana's shoes that had been left to dry by the fireplace. Then, urgently, he began the tedious process of climbing up the sooty passageway. He forced himself to move quickly, because now more than ever, he did not want to be discovered, especially as he could feel a breeze from behind, through the hole in his robe. Climbing from one step to the next, grabbing onto one brick higher with each raised hand, he pulled himself up, up, up. Reaching the top, he scrambled over the rim and made his way back across the roof.

He eased himself down until his feet rested on Cadeau's back. From that position, he lowered himself into the saddle, regretting the burn in his robe for the discomfort it caused to his bare bottom. The horse made little gentle, encouraging noises as its rider resumed his place.

"All right, now go, go!" urged Nicolas, leaning forward to speak the words into the horse's ear.

Just then, Florus emerged from the house. Before the horse could work itself up to a trot and start down the street, the nobleman ran to the side of the priest's mount and grabbed onto Nicolas' sleeve. Nicolas turned to look at the older man, and as by the moon's light Florus saw the blackened, sooty face, he recognized his benefactor at once. He released his hold on the ash-covered robe.

"So it is you!" he exclaimed, breathlessly and gratefully. "I locked the windows and doors, to see if our angel was of flesh and blood after all. How you got in and out is nothing short of a miracle. I see now you are no angel, but a veritable saint."

"Please," urged Nicolas, "tell no one."

With those words, the boy priest gave a fresh command to his steed, which galloped off into the darkness. *If there is a price to be paid for love,* he thought, as the horse carried him through the torch-lit streets, *surely I have paid it in full this night.*

EPILOGUE:

Nico's Departure

News of the Christmas miracle spread like wildfire throughout the city. Though Florus had agreed to tell no one of what had happened, somehow people found out. Fortunately, the name of the boy priest had not yet been linked with the amazing occurrence. Still, by noon of Christmas day, scarcely a man, woman, or child in Patara did not know of the good fortune that had befallen the Dorius family for the third time.

Ana's joy in discovering a sack containing thirty gold pieces hidden in her shoe, less the price of a juicy bone, could scarcely be contained. "It is a miracle!" she exclaimed, over and over. She embraced her father many times and jumped about like a frisky puppy. Then, resolving to run all the way to the inn if necessary, she got no further than the door of the house when the prince burst in to learn whether or not the prayers of the priest had been answered. Her capering and high spirits alone told him the result. Shortly thereafter, Prince Ilyan and his beloved came racing into Father Nicolas' study at the monastery, following the prayer service. Not finding him there, they ran to Abbot Stephanus to tell him the good news.

The Abbot welcomed the tidings with joy, sharing in their great happiness, but he would not permit them to see Father Nicolas.

"It is his prayers that have wrought the miracle!" exclaimed Prince Ilyan.

"Yes, and we want to thank him for remembering us in them," added Ana.

Neither of them yet knew that the giftbringer had in truth been Nicolas, and the Abbot had no intention of revealing the secret. "Father Nicolas will see no one today," he stated, firmly.

Nicolas had retired to his bed too exhausted in body and soul to clean himself. In the morning he had arisen early, bathed, and gotten dressed in a fresh robe. However, even with the soot and ash washed off, his face and limbs remained temporarily scarred and disfigured from the night's adventure. He had cuts, scrapes, abrasions, minor burns, and several bumps and bruises. It would be a long time before he would try another stunt like climbing down a chimney.

Another thing that would not wash off was a feeling of malaise, a sense that he had failed in his mission by being dis-covered at the last. Though his name had not yet been publicly mentioned in connection with the miracle, he feared it would not be long before everyone knew the truth. He did not relish the prospect of being known as a giver of gifts. It would mean everybody would expect something from him, and he had now become the poorest of men, having just given away the last of his wealth.

The boy priest remained in seclusion for a week before he resumed his duties. He then gradually worked himself back into his daily routine. Although he continued to do all of the things he had done before, he had changed. Gone was the light of joy from his grey eyes. Gone was the radiating luster when the sun played with his golden hair. Gone were his warmth, compassion, and friendliness. His smiles, once rare but worth waiting for, had now all but disappeared. Nicolas passed his days going through the motions. He performed marriages. He officiated at funerals. He listened to countless confessions, and offered sound spiritual advice. He preached sermons at mass that stirred the hearts of his congregation. He prayed prayers of great magnificence and beauty, not to mention passionate eloquence reflective of a deep spirituality. Parishioners constantly marveled at the talents of the boy of eighteen. He did all things with excellence, but he did them listlessly, and with only half his heart.

Months passed. Abbot Stephanus' concern increased. Nicolas slept little and ate less. He lost weight. He grew thinner. Dark circles appeared beneath his eyes. He appeared to be wasting away.

"If you continue like this," said the Abbot sternly to his nephew one day, "you will surely die."

"Then I would be grateful," said Nicolas, "for I have nothing more to live for."

"Is this why I made you a priest?" asked the Abbot. "So that you could live a life of despair and gloom? Tell me what is troubling you. Is it this life in the monastery that makes you unhappy? Is your calling not a true calling after all?"

"No, Father," said Nicolas. "I am content in my occupation, but I am weary. I have given, and given, and given until I am spent. I have nothing left to give."

"You have given too much," said the Abbot, dryly. "When you give away all of your heart and hold onto no part of it for yourself, then you have indeed drained yourself out. You are like the Fortunatus purse, perpetually empty."

Nicolas raised an eyebrow, questioningly. "I thought the Fortunatus purse was perpetually full."

"Aha! I've at least got you thinking, and that is a step in the right direction. The purse is both full *and* empty, depending on how you look at it."

"What shall I do, Father? I can find no joy in anything."

"The Lord allows us to be visited with these seasons, from time to time," said Stephanus, sagely. "When you feel low, do not strive *too* hard to feel better, for the more you do the more the good feelings will flee from you."

"Then what is the answer?"

"A sad priest cannot very well bring the joy of the Lord to others," said Stephanus. "I recommend a change of scene. You have lived in this monastery for nine years now, and perhaps it is time for you to see something more of the world."

Nicolas' eyes opened wide at this prospect. It was the first interest he had felt in anything for a long time. "Where would I go?" he asked, almost in awe of his uncle for making such an unexpected suggestion.

"I believe that every churchman should visit Jerusalem and the Holy Lands at least once in his life," said the Abbot. "It would be a good thing for you to travel, and to walk in the places Our Lord walked when He dwelt upon the earth."

"Oh, could I?" asked Nicolas. "That would be an experience beyond anything I have ever dreamed!"

The Abbot's eyes twinkled. "There's my Nico," he said. "There's the young man I know. I hoped I could find you hiding under all of that dark and gloom."

"When could I leave?" asked the boy priest, anxiously.

"As soon as I can arrange passage and write some letters," replied the Abbot.

"Thank you, Father," said Nicolas, with heartfelt conviction.

It didn't take Stephanus long to complete the necessary arrangements. Nicolas was scheduled to set sail from Patara in the early spring. The young priest's life had begun once more to have a sense of meaning and purpose. He again took interest in prayer and contemplation. He fulfilled his duties with a renewed sparkle in his eye.

On the day the boat was to depart, a letter arrived from Petrus. Nicolas read it as he stood with his uncle on the wharf. At the top, the missive bore the name "Father Nicolas," but that name had been scratched out, and beneath it the author had written the more familiar form of address:

Dearest Nico,

I hope this letter reaches you by spring. Abigail is well, although she suffered from a fever when we first arrived in Rome. We have a beautiful villa overlooking the Tiber River. Abigail has made many women friends, which leaves me free to pursue my own pleasures. Though I have lost interest in chariot racing, I still occasionally find time to place wagers on the gladiators in the Colosseum. I have already lost several fortunes in gold pieces, but besides going out, money is coming in as well—at least there is the promise of it. You know that upon my father's death I inherited his position of Senator, and the Senate in Rome is very active just now, so it looks like we won't be returning to Lycia anytime soon. I miss your good friendship and your devotion to God, because they always kept me on the right track. I have no close friends like you here to steady me, although I have discovered that there are a surprising number of Christians in Rome. Here religion is mostly kept quiet though, unless it's worship of the old gods or the official religion of the Empire. Emperor Maximian, Diocletian's co-emperor of the West, is a known enemy of the faith. I hope the tide doesn't turn against Christians anytime soon. Write when you can. I was pleased to learn that Prince Ilyan and Ana are to be married. I hope he finds married life as agreeable as I do. Ha, ha. You know what I mean.

Your friend for life,
Petrus

Nicolas put down the letter. He stood on the wharf facing the city that had been his home since birth. Here he had known untold riches, poverty, deep sorrow, and profound joy. Here his parents lay buried, and here his uncle had raised him. Here he had transformed from a spoiled, selfish child to a holy man of God. Here he had known friendship, fellowship, and even love.

He had truly given everything he could give. He had tried to do it in the name of God and in the name of pure, holy love. The letter in his hand served as a reminder that time had moved on, and so must he. Petrus would always be his friend but as a married man he had to pursue his own course without Nicolas' help. The same held true for the daughters of Florus. They were no longer his responsibility, either. Angelina had married and now lived in the northern country with her husband and child. Abigail had married Nicolas' best friend and gone to Rome. And Ana soon would be married. The wedding date had been set for the spring.

Nicolas had begged to be excused from performing the ceremony, and Stephanus, sagely guessing the reason, had agreed to officiate. Now the issue was no longer a problem, for the ship on which the boy priest would leave for the Holy Lands was to depart three weeks before the wedding of Prince Ilyan and Ana. He would not be present for the occasion.

"Is Petrus well?" asked Abbot Stephanus, who had accompanied Nicolas to the wharf to see his nephew off.

Nicolas smiled briefly. "Petrus is . . . Petrus," he said. "I don't think he will ever really change."

The Abbot put a hand on his nephew's shoulder. "*You* have changed," he said. "You have changed in profound ways. I will never forget the petulant little boy who complained of his parents to me in my study all those years ago. You are not that little boy anymore. Manhood has taught you responsibility, devotion . . . and sacrifice."

Nicolas nodded, painfully aware of that sacrifice.

"Father Nicolas! Father Nicolas!"

Abbot and priest looked up. Ana came running along the wharf toward them.

Nicolas' first impulse was to get on board the ship right away, but Stephanus held him by the sleeve. "Talk to her," encouraged the Abbot.

"I—I—" stammered the boy priest.

"Talk to her," said Stephanus, firmly. The Abbot withdrew to a discreet distance while Ana approached Nicolas.

The young woman's long unbound hair flowed behind her as she ran, and when she came close to the young priest, it fell about her face in uncombed strands and tangles. Her cheeks were red and flushed, her green eyes glinting with eager recognition of an old friend, while a mysterious, sly, catlike smile lit up her face. "I came as soon as I learned you were leaving," she gasped, trying to catch her breath now that she had stopped running.

"Yes, the ship sets sail in a few minutes," said Nicolas. "I will visit Bethlehem and Jerusalem and other places where Our Lord lived and walked."

"You look as though this is something you really want," said Ana, wistfully.

"It is. And you are to be married in a few weeks," said Nicolas, trying not to let his voice tremble as he said the words. "It is my hope and prayer that you—and Prince Ilyan—will find much happiness together."

"Yes," said Ana, a little too brightly, a little too earnestly. "Of course we will."

The bustle on the wharf slowed as the crewmen, having loaded all the cargo, boarded the ship and prepared for imminent departure.

"I—I must get on board the ship," said Nicolas, nervously. "It looks like it is about to sail. Farewell, dearest Ana." Trembling in every fiber of his being as he steeled himself to take leave of her, he leaned forward stiffly and formally to deliver a priestly kiss on her forehead. Then, unable to bear the strain of

being in her presence any longer, he turned and walked reso-
lutely away, to take a final leave of the Abbot and then to get
aboard.

"Nico!" Her shriek flew to his ears, carried by the
Mediterranean breeze. He turned to see her running toward him.
She flung herself into his embrace, sobbing as if her heart would
break. "Nico, please, don't go. Or if you must, take me with
you!"

He looked at her in mingled alarm and joy, gently caressing her as she sobbed in his arms. He didn't know what to say.
So—she loved him, after all! That part had not been purely his
imagination. Yet did he love her sufficiently to forsake his vows?
Now that the test had come he felt woefully unprepared.

"I've sensed all along that I loved you," confessed Ana,
her eyes brimming with tears. "Since I first saw you on the day
of that ill-fated chariot race, and later, as you grew and lived
at the monastery, I followed the progress of your career with
a great deal of interest. The day you became a priest I was
reminded again of how impressed I had always been with you.
You seemed so Christ-like and godly, up there on the platform,
that I could not take my eyes off of you. But since I knew you
belonged to God, I felt that Ilyan must have been the one God
intended for me. He—he loves me dearly, would do anything
for me, would die for me. And I love him, I do, but not as I have
loved you! Papa told me, you see—Papa told me everything!
How it was you who left the gifts of the dowries on Christmas
Eve, how it was you who clambered down our chimney and covered yourself with soot and ash just so that I could become a
bride. I swore that I would always love our benefactor, our good
angel—and it was you!"

He held her and hugged her, not minding or caring that
he did it under Father Stephanus' watchful eye. With his thumbs
and fingers, he wiped the tears from Ana's cheeks. "I love you,
too," he murmured. There! He had said it! He had confessed his

love to the girl he adored. But was this his absolute, irrevocable choice? He didn't know.

"I cannot marry Ilyan, I cannot," said Ana. "He knows I do not love quite as much as he and it seems not to bother him. He tells me I will learn to love him more, and he will teach me. But it is not a lesson I want to learn. It is you, my Nico, who holds my heart."

"Never did I dream that I would hear those words from your lips, my beloved Ana," said Nicolas. He resolved at that moment to renounce his vows, to leave the priesthood, and to marry the woman he loved and be a man like any other. It was what he had longed for. What he had lived for. What he had prayed for.

He leaned down to press his lips to hers, to seal their love with a passionate lover's kiss, to separate himself once and for all from the vocation to which he had long ago been called. But he paused before their lips touched, his mouth poised in readiness, stopping inches short of making the desired contact. He found that he could not kiss her.

Something stood in his way.

It was not the presence of Abbot Stephanus, who had doubtless witnessed many such scenes in his lifetime and was not likely to be shocked or scandalized. It was not the distant calls of one of the crewmen for the passengers to get aboard. It was not the fact that the woman in his arms had given her pledge to marry another man. It was something far greater, far more powerful.

It was the Lord.

Go thou, and deliver My gifts to the world.

Nicolas knew then that God had further purposes for him, and further gifts for him to give. He realized with finality that he could not veer away from the course the Lord had set for him without untold misery and hardship. Through God's will and God's choosing had Nicolas been made a priest and the priesthood was not to be mocked or taken lightly. The boy priest had understood when he had taken his vows how binding and irrevocable they were, but it was not mere earthly vows made before men that kept him bound to his promise. His own sense of devotion, of rightness, of what he knew, yes *knew,* beyond any doubt that God wanted of him—that was what called to him now. Having lived within the will of God for so long, he now realized that in his heart he had no desire to live outside of it. A priest he had become, and a priest he had to remain. This was another of the sacrifices that God expected him to make.

"No, Ana," he said, at length. "It is wrong. I cannot break my vows. You must not break your pledge to Ilyan. He needs you, and there is a world waiting out there that needs me. We cannot forsake our destinies just to satisfy our own desires."

"Oh, dear, dear Nico, no!" protested Ana, sobbing as he broke away from her.

"It must be," he said. "I am a priest. You are very close to becoming a bride. You must go where you are needed. Go to the man who has given his heart to you. Love him, and make him happy. You and I could never know a moment's joy if it meant betraying one who has been a good friend to each of us. We could never know peace if we knew that we had forsaken the will of the Lord." He could hardly believe it was himself saying those words, yet he knew in his heart that what he spoke was the truth.

Ana sank to her knees, weeping openly. "What can I do?" she sobbed. "What can I do?"

Nicolas said gently, "You will keep your promises. And so will I."

"I do not love him as I love you."

"And that is as it should be. Don't you see? The love you have for me is like the love one has for God or the things of the church. You have mistaken it for passion because your devotion is so intense. There are few young women who have such a deep love for all things that are good, holy, and pure. At first I tried to fool myself into thinking that your great love was for me, as a man, but you were seeing past me, to the things I represented. It is God you love, and it is He for whom you feel such strong feelings. Do you understand? It is only just and fitting that your love for the Lord should overwhelm any feelings you may have of ordinary human love. As for Prince Ilyan, you must follow your heart, but I think you really love him. I think you love him as a woman loves a man. I have little doubt that his love for you is genuine. It is he with whom you will find true happiness. I say this, not because it gives me any pleasure, but because it is the truth."

His soft answer seemed to have its effect. She stopped crying, and with some difficulty managed to dry her tears. She stood up and faced him, her green eyes now tinged with red. "You are right, of course, Father Nicolas," she said, her voice still choking from the recent torrents of emotion. Her words, however, were calm and even. "You are so young, scarcely older than myself," said Ana. "A boy who was not of God would have run away with me, and brought me to ultimate shame and disgrace. A boy who was not of God would not have sacrificed his own love by delivering a gift that made it possible for another to marry me." She nodded, slowly. "I know your feelings are as great as mine. And I know the kind of love for God of which you speak. Because of the love I bear for you and for Him, but also out of my own heart, I will do as you say. I will go to Ilyan. I will wed him. I will love him in every possible way. I will be the best and most loving wife he could have. I do love him, you know. I was just blinded momentarily by—by the light. You are wise and good, and I am grateful for your excellent counsel. But," she whispered, "I will always have a special love for you."

"I will always love you in a special way as well," said Father Nicolas. "A priest may love," he murmured, as though understanding it for the first time himself, "and it can be a right and holy love, as long as he obeys and remains faithful to God. I now know, as I have always known but not admitted, that I love you in a way that transcends earthly love, in the way that God wants us all to love one another. But it is much more than that, for you will always occupy a place of honor in my heart."

Another call came for passengers to get aboard.

He took her in his arms one more time, both instinctively knowing it would be their last embrace together on this earth. Now that the course was set, and known, it was easier for him to hold her. He relished this final, unambiguous moment more than any other they had shared together. Understanding and acceptance had created an unbreakable bond between them. He held onto her until, overcome with emotion, she finally pulled away, backing one step at a time. At arm's length, their hands broke apart, and she stood looking at him, as though trying to engrave his face forever on her memory.

Nicolas, too, savored his last look at the young woman who might have been his one and only earthly love. Both knew that they would never again truly be apart, no matter how many miles or how many circumstances separated them. And both knew in their hearts that the painful choice they had made was the right and godly one.

"Farewell," said Ana. "Farewell, Father Nicolas. And farewell to you, Abbot Stephanus," she called, a little more loudly. Then to Nicolas, she said, fervently, "Thank you. Thank you for being the giftbringer."

"God gave the gifts," said Nicolas. "I was but His means of delivering them."

She gave him one last, lingering gaze. Touching her fingers to her lips, she raised and waved them in the gesture of blowing a kiss. Then she turned away, walking at a brisk pace and not looking back, and within moments she had melted into the crowd that bustled about the shipyards.

Nicolas returned to his uncle's side. "It was not an easy choice to make," said Stephanus. "It never is. But some day you will realize it was more than worth it."

"I feel as though a great burden has lifted from my heart," said Nicolas. "I thought I would be sad and miserable, but now that I have made my choice I feel at peace. Still, I suppose I have said farewell to my chances of ever really being a man."

"On the contrary, nephew," said Abbot Stephanus, "you have only now truly become a man."

After giving the Abbot a final farewell embrace, Father Nicolas managed to reach the ship just before the gangplank was to be removed from the pier. Despite his hurry, he carried himself with a certain grace and dignity. Mounting the ramp, he lifted the skirts of his robes to facilitate his progress up the incline, moving with the unconscious elegance of one nobly born, even though limping slightly on his left leg. He wore an expression of exhilaration by the time he reached the top. His every muscle seemed to quiver with the anticipation of adventure, of the excitement of experiencing new sights and new sounds. He waved to his uncle from the deck of the boat.

Standing at the end of the wharf, Abbot Stephanus watched the boat set sail. He reflected on the change he now beheld in his nephew. The young man needed to get away, to forget the sorrows of his youth and develop a deeper sense of the purpose of his calling. The Abbot regretted the parting, but recognized his nephew's need for wider horizons. Stephanus knew that the lessons begun by his brother during Nicolas' childhood, and continued under his own guidance in the monastery, were far from over. Life, the greatest teacher of all, had more education in store for the young priest who in turn had much to give to others. The Abbot wondered how long it would be before he saw Nicolas again, knowing full well that it might be never. This caused his heart to ache with sadness, though he knew the time had come to let his nephew go. God would take care of the young man, this Stephanus did not doubt.

Slowly the craft pulled away from the pier. The Abbot waved to the golden-haired, black-robed figure on the deck. The boy priest energetically waved back. As the folds of the robe fluttered in the sea breeze, a sunbeam caught the tangled, windblown strands of golden hair and bathed them in a radiant glow.

Stephanus kept his eye on the boat as it diminished into the distance, until the blue Mediterranean waves had carried it out of his sight.